# Earthly Needs

MARTY DAMON

January 2017

*To my husband, who knew me as a teenager*

*and who has been with me every step of the way.*

*also*

*To all my supportive fellow writers of*

*the Monday night and Wednesday morning gangs*

*and*

*To my kind and skilled editor, Claire Hopley*

# CHAPTER ONE

It was the end of first period and Lila Wallace was just beginning to present the homework assignment to the protesting faces before her when she heard a loud thump against the heavy brown classroom door. This was followed by a great scuffling and shrieking. Her 10th grade English class reacted as one, preparing to leap to their feet and investigate. One thing you could usually depend in an urban high school was plenty of excitement, thought Lila. "Sit!" she commanded on her way to the door. At the end of the corridor she would have sworn she saw Assistant Principal Paschetti, but then whoever it was vanished as quickly as virtue at a senior prom.

She turned her attention to the backpacks and jackets that lay on the hallway floor as if some new molting season had begun. In the middle was a tangle of two very angry girls, shouting loud and redundant obscenities, and on the outside, five teenage onlookers who had happened to be passing by and now were enjoying every minute of the entertainment. Jerome Sweetwater, the beloved and aging assistant principal, was preparing to jump into the fray. As usual, he was nattily turned out in a well-tailored suit, but his lined brown face was grim. Lila hoped she'd been mistaken in her sighting of Paschetti. Even he wouldn't have deliberately left Jerome to deal with this on his own – or would he? Lila pulled her classroom door shut behind her and moved in to help. Her neighbor in 304, Bill Moynihan, a rumpled fatherly figure and thankfully, a large one, came out of his room.

Oh my God, thought Lila, nothing worse than a girl fight. Why couldn't it have been a couple of football players? That would have been much easier to handle.

Both veteran teachers, and both aware they didn't want Sweetwater in the thick of the skirmish, Lila and Bill moved together into the front lines. He pulled away the first combatant in somewhat ragged pink and purple, with matching pink hair. Lila restrained the second, who was in an ensemble enlivened by generous helpings of gold in several forms: beading, embroidery, and sequins. His captive was still putting on a good show, but seemed to be flagging, while Lila's detainee was incredibly small and incredibly angry, her heeled boots slashing the air in her opponent's direction as Lila held her, arms around the middle. Mr. Sweetwater stepped forward and the police officer stationed in the building hurried down the hall in their direction. "Thanks, you two. Sorry to have interrupted your classes."

As the smaller of the two girls was handed off to the police, she coolly reached out to one of the bystanders, who returned to her a necklace spelling out "Izzy" in gold, along with two huge gold hoop earrings. So, thought Lila, she must have been the attacker. The tiny fireball had had the foresight to remove any jewelry that might have been damaged in the fray. The second girl, much subdued, but with ear-shattering sobs that tested the strength of the glass in each classroom door, followed the first pair down the hall in the custody of Mr. Sweetwater.

"Well, that's that," said Lila to Bill. "And it's not even second period yet. This is shaping up to be an interesting day."

"Good moves there, Lila. Fast footwork and restraining holds should be a required course in teacher training classes."

"You weren't too shabby yourself. And you know how it is; nothing's more annoying than finally getting your class on track and then being interrupted. I'll do anything for a quiet hallway."

Lila and Bill turned back to their rooms just as the bell rang and students raced out of all classroom doors, not so much motivated to get to the next class as to have more quality hall time. Damn! thought Lila. I never gave them the homework. Now they'll be behind my other two tenth grade classes.

She grabbed a pen to make a large red reminder of this fact in her planning book. Paschetti stuck his ferret-like face in the door. "Heard you had some excitement up here. Disappointing to learn of such behavior in your portion of the third floor." He was clutching his treasured badge of rank, a walkie-talkie, and there was an unattractive gleam in his eye. Here is a man who probably slows down to get the full enjoyment out of traffic accidents, thought Lila. And by the way, how was she supposed to prevent hall fights when she was in her room teaching?

"It was over in about five minutes, Mr. Paschetti. A lot of bluster and noise. Just sound and fury, signifying nothing."

"So Jerome was up here helping? I'd say he's a little past dealing with that kind of event." There was a bubble of spittle in the corner of Paschetti's mouth.

"Nope, Mr. Sweetwater did just fine, a key element to our success." She continued to shuffle papers on her desk, looking busy in order to keep the conversation brief. Jerome Sweetwater was one of a dying breed: a good administrator whose kindness was legendary. Lila was damned if she'd give this upstart the satisfaction of being right. Paschetti's recent trajectory from business teacher to assistant principal at Thomas Paine High was still suspect. She knew there had been rumors about Principal Galaska having a hand in his promotion. Some people had even suggested that Paschetti had a hold over her. Something about her having changed the results from her last school's standardized tests. Paschetti had been a teacher at that school when Galaska had been there as principal, but Lila still found it hard to believe that even he was slimy enough to stoop to blackmail, or that Thelma would alter student scores for her own benefit. Not that in a city filled with schools identified as 'failing' some principals wouldn't be sorely tempted to fiddle with the state standardized tests. Student results often determined an administrator's salary or even if they were going to retain their job.

Paschetti tapped the door frame jauntily. "Just wish I'd been here to lend a hand, particularly after my recent course on intervention strategies."

"Uh huh," said Lila, remembering the distant figure in the hallway.

He stood in the doorway, clearly burning to share with her his endless knowledge. Lila finished stacking papers and sat down at her computer, mouse in hand, looking pointedly at the screen. He tapped another tattoo on the door frame and finally caught the lack of encouragement from her. "Well, duty calls!" and he marched off.

She swiveled her chair to stare out the window into the fall sunshine and consider Paschetti's obvious ambition. Was his possible avoidance of the fight an example of cowardice or instead maybe the hope that Jerome wouldn't be up to the task? Hard to say. It was all well and good to have goals, but his seemed unhealthy, likely to have their roots in others' misfortune. And what was he hoping for anyway? He'd only been an assistant principal for about eight months, and to Lila's knowledge, Principal Galaska had no plans to leave.

Lila shook her head and returned to her planning. Paschetti was a living example of why the best part of her job was when she could close her classroom door and it was just her and her kids. Teaching was challenging enough without having to deal with all these political machinations.

\*\*\*

The last bell finally rang but Lila still had one student who stopped by to pick up a past assignment, a second from the year before who came to boast about the A he'd received from this year's English class, and a third who just wanted a room to hang out in while she waited for her boyfriend taking a make-up test next door. Lila explained, congratulated, and shooed, hoping to get out of work while her students were still teenagers.

Now that she was at last behind the wheel, she decided to take a different route. Driving the same path day after day sometimes made her feel like a hamster on a treadmill. A more scenic view might help her clear her head and transition from her day at school.

The road she turned onto was still in the city, but near its border, and the occasional clumps of trees increased until soon she was passing small wooded areas. The trees were large and looked to have been there for some time. Next came a big white farmhouse that had somehow survived in spite of the tract of boxy houses in back of it and the filling station to its right. To its side was a huge yard, more of a field, actually, that encompassed perhaps as much as two acres. She wondered how much longer it would be here, this quiet reminder of big families and simpler lives.

Her car drew closer to the house and she saw a sign hidden by a sprawling patch of bushes. Its picture of a beaming family proclaimed that this would soon be the site of another Home and Family Bank, and in the distance sat a hulking yellow bulldozer under a wide-limbed oak as if to underscore that fact. More development, thought Lila. How many banks do we need, anyway? Soon that beautiful old home will be balanced on a small scrap of land, next to an asphalted parking lot where once there had been tomatoes or corn. Moving back to her hometown of Calvin three years ago had awakened the Theroux within her. As much as she'd enjoyed her spell of city living, it was the trees and fields that renewed her. She drove on, thinking she was glad that, so far at least, Calvin had had the sense to guard its remaining open spaces from disappearing forever.

A few minutes later Lila pulled into her driveway and sat, letting the afternoon quiet wash over her. She put her head back and dropped her tired shoulders, tasting the breeze as much as feeling it. After a few minutes she got out and walked up the drive to the mailbox, sorting through the flyers and bills on her way back, leaving them next to her briefcase and lunch bag on the bench by the door. Having been stuck in a classroom for hours, it was too nice an afternoon to go inside yet. She wandered over her yard, picking a tomato she had missed the day before along with some too-long pole beans hiding beneath their leaves. Near the house a silent deer was contentedly chewing up one of her hosta plants. The doe turned her big cocoa eyes toward her, barely moving even when Lila waved both arms wildly as though signaling for help from a distant ship. Fine, thought Lila. It had been a long day. The hosta would grow back. She gathered up her things and went into the quiet farmhouse.

10

Dealing with a hundred and twenty teenagers every day did not allow for many moments of contemplation and as she dropped her belongings in the kitchen she told herself she should be grateful for this solitude. Out of the kitchen window she could see the peach tree where she had spent so many childhood hours reading. Her father, a college professor, and her mother, a jewelry designer, had been so wrapped up in their work and each other that she had by necessity been more self-contained than other children. Oh sure, her parents had always been kind, but it had been a kindness of benign inattention. Her father's study and her mother's studio had felt like vaguely unwelcome places to her. Her memories of physical affection from her parents were few, and it had sometimes occurred to Lila that perhaps this was the cause of both her occasional impetuous romances and her gift for dodging anything deeper.

Her last relationship had been longer than others. It had probably made it as far as it did because they'd kept it carefree and undemanding, the shared experience of two urban professionals simply enjoying life. It was when she and Craig had moved to Calvin that things began to fall apart. Nothing like a quiet evening in a small town to make you focus on that person across the kitchen table and think about those other many quiet evenings ahead.

She kicked aside these dreary thoughts along with her school shoes and
padded upstairs barefoot to change into running gear. Soon she was out on Old County Road, headed away from town. She needed to empty her head and just listen to the sound of her sneakers on the

road. She jogged along, undisturbed by traffic. It was a pleasure to indulge in a mid-afternoon run while the commuters were still in their offices. This was definitely one of the perks of teaching, in spite of the endless grading or the fact that you couldn't go to the rest room when nature called.

This stretch of road was bordered mostly by fields and patches of woods, more evidence that the town was managing to keep heavy development at bay. Soon she came up to the railroad crossing; the tracks were used less and less, but when she was in bed she could heard the whistle of a late-night train. They still looked viable, practically as good as when they had carried grain and feed to supply the many farms that had once been the backbone of Calvin. All but a few of the farms were now gone and the trains were more likely to carry commuters on their way to Boston.

A glance down the rail line showed no train, but she did see a figure walking along the tracks about a fourth of a mile away. She jogged in place, wondering who it might be. She wouldn't have been surprised to see kids there. Something about railroad tracks seemed to draw them. But this was a grown man, solidly built, and presentably dressed in a blue shirt that contrasted with his dark blond hair. Not a vagrant, she thought. Probably someone surveying the land or something. To what purpose, she wondered? She turned, leaving the man and her questions behind, another two miles still to cover between her and a well-earned early dinner.

Clouds gathered in the distance and the rumble of thunder speeded her steps.

# CHAPTER TWO

The next day the sun was still on its way up and a not-quite stocky, but powerfully built man stood on the newly-added porch that wrapped around two sides of his house. In his mid-forties, he exemplified the expression, "prime of life." His face was tan, his hair curly and blond, and his slightly hooded grey eyes appeared to miss nothing before him. His feet were planted wide and solid, as though he were standing on the deck of a ship. He rested his large hands on the railing, his wide shoulders shifting while he scanned the land before him. His land. The recently cropped field reached for quite a distance before connecting with the line of trees. His breathing was even and steady, that of a man in control. These acres were now his and he had plans for them, changes for the land and the town, changes that he knew from past experience in other towns might require some finesse with his neighbors.

\*\*\*

Down Old County Road, Lila was clean and dressed, about her only sartorial goal at this hour. She put in the last earring and ran downstairs. From long habit formed after that growth spurt at thirteen, she ducked her head at the bottom step, narrowly missing the low beam above the final riser in the old house. In the kitchen she found her purse and overstuffed briefcase on the window seat, heaved them to her shoulder, pulled her lunch from the fridge, and grabbed her umbrella from the counter.

She turned to leave and there sat her big gray tomcat Winston. Would she ever remember to close off the cat door?

"Winston! I've told you, no friends inside!"

What looked to be a five pound squirrel stared fatalistically at her from the hunter's mouth. A beat of five seconds passed as all parties froze. Then came a sudden rush of activity as Lila and Winston dodged and weaved, he with the squirrel, she with the umbrella, first with a feint left, a lunge right, until she finally drove him back to the enclosed porch and shut the house door.

Lila stood for a moment, catching her breath. Apparently Winston had now officially killed all the chipmunks in a five mile radius and had moved on to squirrels. What would be next? Portly woodchucks pushed in from behind? It was great to be loved so absolutely, something she had yet to experience in human form, but she wished this love didn't manifest itself in live - or too often - dead offerings.

Cautiously she slipped through the door to avoid letting the cat in for round two. She would have to deal with the squirrel, or what remained of him, when she got back from school. She walked to her car, dodging a few puddles from last night's downpour. Still a little rattled from her duel, she piled briefcase, lunch, purse, and umbrella in the back seat next to the plastic grocery bag of classroom supplies she'd left there. A large drip from the tree above traveled down her neck as she climbed into the driver's seat. Not the most auspicious way to begin her day.

She glanced at her reflection in the rear view mirror, startled by the improvement over the Lila who had stumbled into the shower. Even in her early forties, she was still amazed at the difference a little, although grudging, effort on her part could achieve.

She reached the end of her driveway and glanced across the quiet six a.m. road. She saw that someone had recently cleared the two acre field on the other side. It was part of the old Wetherill farm that had finally been put up for sale after the last surviving relative lost interest. She looked over the remaining summer tiger lilies edging Old County Road and wondered if someone had indeed bought the property. The house itself was a distance from the road, and therefore not exactly a next-door neighbor. Still, it would be good to have someone there who cared about the place again. She hoped it would be someone who, like her, respected the beauty of this town with its woods and fields.

***

Up the road, Sam Fielding had been sitting in his kitchen, lacing up his shoes for a run to the center of town. The two plus miles to get there were no problem. In his early fifties, his body had grown strong from staying active and working his land. Now, though, he wondered if he needed so much land, wondered if it was time for a change.

He reached down to tie the next shoe, his lanky arms strong and brown from hours in his garden. He planned to stop by the market to pick up some of that good ground coffee they carried there, and he also needed . . . . He paused; the lace to his second shoe still untied in his hand, and he looked blankly out the screen door to his front yard. What was the other thing he needed? Damn. Lately, thoughts that had sat solidly in his mind one minute would now too often dissolve into vapor, refusing to return to any sort of concrete form. Well, it might come back to him when he got there. At the very least, he'd clear his head with a run and perhaps have a chance for a little conversation.

Some time had now gone by since May, his wife of nearly thirty years, had died, and while he still missed her desperately, his need for solitude was slowly being replaced by another one - a need for companionship. He finished tying his shoe, not without difficulty. Along with memory issues, his fingers didn't seem to want to cooperate lately either. He left the house, deadheading the tiger lilies along his driveway as he walked and then speeded to a jog.

\*\*\*

Lila and Sam's new neighbor shrugged on a field jacket and started across his land. The grass was still wet with morning dew so he chose a deer path running parallel with the road on the other side of the overgrowth. He knew his property line wasn't far from his house. He had walked it with the realtor a few months back, but now he wanted another look.

He first heard the rhythmic sound of shoes hitting pavement, the steady gait of a jogger. He walked on, and even a businessman like him couldn't help noting the play of morning light and the freshness of the air. A few minutes later came the low murmur of an engine, noticeable in the early-morning quiet. He looked through the patch of small trees to his right and saw a woman pull out of the driveway across the road. His glance through her windshield, and then side window as she turned, told him this was a neighbor he was interested in meeting. Very interested. Her deep chestnut hair gleamed, framed by the yellowing leaves of a sugar maple, and then she was gone. With her departure, his mind turned to thoughts of zoning, access roads, and availability to the rail lines that edged his property. He continued down the path and came to the stake that delineated the edge of his land. He noted the stretch of his field and how it met his neighbor's – what was the name? Fielding? How very appropriate.

*****

Unaware that she was one of those neighbors the big man on the porch was planning to charm, or even that her thoughts about a neighbor had become a reality, Lila turned on to Old County Road and headed to the center of Calvin. It was a short drive, and in a matter of minutes she was parked in front of Binding-Stevens Market, the small store in the village center. This crossroads, like so many others in New England, held a statue, a gazebo, a smattering of commercial buildings, and was edged by pre-Civil War and a few pre-Revolutionary War white frame houses. The creaking wood porch of the store in the old red building belied the fact that inside was a state of the art cappuccino machine installed to lure the town's young professionals. These newcomers were either restoring the two-hundred-year –old colonials in town or building fifteen- room testaments to their wealth up on Calvin Mountain. The town council was caught in a delicate dance between welcoming new tax revenue and preserving the land.

Lila entered the old building; the store was busy, as it usually was at this hour. The tables to her right were filled, as patrons with more flexible schedules settled in with newspapers and coffee. She paid for her tea, nodded to a couple of people she knew and left, ducking under the still-blooming white clematis vine that grew along the edge of the porch overhang. She placed her cup on top of her car and opened the door, unlocked, like most in town, and tossed her purse into the passenger seat.

Sam emerged onto the white-trimmed porch of the village store just as Lila reached across her car to get her tea. She had glanced over quickly and so he didn't register at first as someone she knew. Her mind automatically filed him into the handsome-tall-athletic category, and she had instinctively sucked in her stomach and put her hand up to check her hair.

Wait - it's just Sam, she told herself. What was the matter with her?

He came down the steps holding a small bag and grinned when he saw her. Sam was no relation, but he was practically a member of her family nonetheless. It seemed he had lived down the road from her parents' house – now hers – for as long as she could remember. For Pete's sake. Here was no romantic target. If ever there was a person she could relax and be herself with, it was Sam.

She returned his smile, saying, "Hey, Sam, how are you this morning?"

It was good to see him smiling. She thought he had grown increasingly distracted over the past couple of years. Maybe it was the result of depression since May's death. Nevertheless, he still had that air of command from his days as the town of Calvin's high school principal. His thick graying hair and erect frame added dignity to his running shorts and t-shirt.

"Delilah Lee! Shouldn't you be at school?"

Lila winced. She hoped Sam was the only person who recalled her full name, a misguided combination of her father's love of old-fashioned names and her mother's southern roots. "No, Sam, it's not even 6:30 yet and I even have a little time to spare. Would you like a lift back to your house?"

"I'd enjoy that if you have time. In this weather, the run down was a pleasure, but we could catch up a little on the return trip. And maybe retracing my steps will jog my memory. I had a few more things to pick up here at the market, but they seem to have slipped my mind."

"Tell you what. I'll call you from school this afternoon just before I leave. I have some errands of my own, so I can pick up whatever you want, too."

"All right, but in exchange, come by for dinner tonight. I'll fix us something fresh from my garden. None of that packaged food everyone poisons themselves with nowadays."

Sam opened the door on his side, sat, and waited while Lila settled her tea in the cup holder. She pulled out of her parking place and headed back. He slapped his thighs as a thought occurred to him. "Don't forget to bring Craig tonight for dinner. He and I need to catch up on our chess games. It's been days since we've played."

What was the matter with him? Lila glanced away from the road in quiet exasperation. "It's been longer than that. Don't you remember? He moved back down to Washington three months ago."

When Lila had left Washington to care for her ailing parents, Craig had left his D.C. real estate business to join her. But like too many times before, she had grown skittish. Her reluctance to discuss any permanent arrangement and his impatience with the slower pace of life in Calvin finally took their toll. After months of shared misery, he'd left.

Sam turned in his seat and stared at her blankly for a moment. He rubbed his long fingers across his chin and then stared back out of the windshield. "Oh, Li, that's right – What was I thinking? I thought of chess and the idea just popped into my head -"

"Don't worry about it. And if it's chess you want, then chess you'll get. Break out your board because you and I will be putting it to good use tonight."

On Old County Road, Sam and Lila traveled in the companionable silence of long-time friends until they reached the cluster of neighborhood mailboxes, triggering a thought for Lila. "What's up at the Wetherills', Sam? Will we be seeing some new neighbors soon? Do you know anything about them?"

"Arlene at the real estate office says the new owner is a single man who claims he wants to get away from the city. I don't know, though. I think it's odd for a single person to decide to move out here."

"Well, you never know – maybe he's a writer or an artist of some kind. Aren't they always supposed to be seeking quiet?"

"It's anything but quiet over there with the sounds of hammering and machinery I've been hearing. As for his occupation, Arlene says he's into some kind of finance - mergers and such."

"Then I'm out of theories. We'll just have to wait and see."

She spotted the gray split-rail fence that marked the beginning of Sam's driveway. She signaled left to the still empty road, and started down the long drive, past his seemingly endless vegetable patch. "Your crops are looking really strong this year."

Eggplants jostled with beans, cucumbers spilled over their trellises, pumpkin vines trailed into the neighboring grass: Sam had thrown himself into gardening after May's death. It had seemed to give his life some purpose and his neighbors reaped the benefits of his over-enthusiastic zucchini vines or a bumper crop of tomatoes. In addition, he had found another new interest in his passionate adoption of a fully vegan diet over the past two years.

"It was a good year for growing. I'll be busy blanching and freezing the next few weeks. And of course delivering the extras around town."

They pulled up to the comfortable gray cottage. Signs of May were still there: an empty basket by the door that she had used to collect roses, the hefty stick to quell any local dogs on her daily walks, and, typical of the quirky May, under the porch settee the roller blades from her healthier days.

Sam telescoped up to his full height, well over six feet, and leaned in the car window. His blue eyes, now sharp and alert, smiled into hers. Damn, thought Lila, he's a handsome guy, not to mention the swimmer's build that had brought him all those still-unbroken swimming records. They'd grown increasingly close over the past couple of years as they supported each other through the heartache of loss – for Lila, her parents, and of course for Sam, his wife.

"Now don't you gorge yourself on roast beef sandwiches at lunch. There'll be bruschetta and beer here at 5:00."

"Sam, in spite of what you think with that vegan mind of yours, we don't exactly sit around at school gnawing on sides of beef. Most of us are die-hard yogurt eaters; we don't have time for much else."

"The milk for that yogurt had to be produced by a fellow creature. I'd rather hear you're all sitting down to tossed salads."

Lila put the car into reverse, "We're not going to get into a meat and morality debate at this hour. I'll see you later."

Sam gave a friendly thump to her roof as he straightened, and waved as she backed away. It really was a shame he was retired, she thought; he'd been an excellent principal. She knew the Calvin school board had tried to persuade him to stay, but he had wanted to spend with May every moment of whatever time she had left. He'd argued that a leave of absence would be unfair to the person hired as the temporary principal. He had put a good face on it, talking of all the projects he'd have time for now, rather than the fact that he'd be spending most of that time at May's bedside.

Now Lila reflected that in light of Sam's wandering focus, perhaps it was just as well that he'd retired?

# CHAPTER THREE

She was late. She was never late.

Lila turned at Calvin's center of town and headed into the city. The traffic was an entirely different animal now; it was amazing what a difference fifteen or twenty minutes could make in her commute. As she drove, the scenery went from trees interspersed with the occasional house to houses interspersed with the occasional tree.

As the landscaped changed, so did her thoughts. Musings about land, neighbors, and Sam turned to her day ahead at school. Then she was in the city proper, with kids in their gangsta outfits at the bus stops, and the MacDonald's workers beginning the morning shift.

She tilted her head slightly to avoid the ricochet of the rising sun in her rear-view mirror. Her focus had become single-minded – shaving every possible moment off her commute to work. She cut in front of one last car at the stop light, took a right into the parking lot of Thomas Paine High School – pretending not to see her colleague who was trying to enter from the opposite direction – and pulled into one of the two remaining spots. Other late-comers, usually the younger teachers whose social lives prevented them arriving until the last bell was ringing, would have to park on the street. Off-campus parking didn't just mean a longer walk to the building. In this neighborhood it often meant that something might be missing by mid-afternoon – the radio, the battery, or perhaps the entire car.

She arrived with what felt like only a handful of minutes before the bell and was mildly shaken by this blip in her routine. She pulled her school ID on its chain from the console and hung it around her neck. The photo matched the face above it: chestnut hair, temporarily reined in at least for the moment with a sturdy barrette, amber eyes punctuated slightly by one or two wrinkles. With her strong cheek bones and wide grin, it was not only a friendly face, but some might say a beautiful one.

The crowd ahead of her parted with all the eager cooperation of a herd of sheep blocking an Irish country lane. She plowed through the assembled bodies, trying not to hear the various conversations. It wasn't just her love of a good parking spot that made her arrive long before her students. She preferred the classroom version of them rather than the one they presented to the world when they were trash talking with their friends.

"Yo, Miss." Brandon, always unfailingly polite, paused in his conversation and gave her a head nod as she went by.

"Good morning, Brandon. See you later." He was in her third period but would inevitably arrive late with his excuse du jour.

Doreen Nauman, who was the shining light of the school's track team, and as usual, surrounded by admirers, waved briefly, and then turned back to her entourage.

They were a study in contrasts: the boys were in clothes so baggy it was a mystery why they didn't just slide off into puddles of denim on the ground, while the girls' outfits were apparently spray-painted on. Trevor, the bane of her existence in period six, finished a complicated handshake with a friend and raised a free hand in her direction. She had found over years of teaching, that it was often the 'bad boys' who won her heart in spite of the challenges they brought.

She pulled the heavy old door open and found her least-favorite person positioned on the other side. Standing there, clipboard in hand, was Anthony Paschetti, assistant principal extraordinaire – just ask him, she thought to herself. He was compiling a list of teachers who'd arrived late, a spiteful task that would never have occurred to the school's other assistant principals. As much as she would have like to pretend he wasn't there, she decided she'd make an attempt at collegiality.

"Good morning, Mr. Paschetti."

"Good morning, Miss Wallace." He pointedly looked at his watch and then made a check mark on his list, a tight smile raising just the corners of his purse-like mouth. Seeing him might be a blot on her morning, but her tardiness had certainly brightened his.

A boy ran toward, and then past them both, bumping Lila's shoulder as he turned the corner to the hall on their left. Pushed toward Paschetti, she quickly steadied her footing and watched the student as he traveled at top speed down the hall. He was hitting lockers with his fist as he went, in what looked to be rage rather than high spirits. An older teacher coming out of her classroom just missed being knocked down. Lila looked over at Paschetti, expecting him to intervene, but he was studiously ignoring the entire incident. Great, thought Lila. Good to know things are under control here.

She headed for the main office on the first floor. Once there, she picked up the key for her classroom, spotting Principal Galaska in her office, already looking as though she'd put in a full day. Lila hoped those rumors about Thelma's heart condition were just that. She was a good principal and the school couldn't afford to lose her.

In the mail room she pulled out the contents of the cubbyhole labeled with her name, sorted most of it right into the trash barrel by the door, and then started up the stairs. Her briefcase was beginning its annoying slide down her left shoulder with each step, pulling her purse with it and grazing the stairs as she climbed. She leaned to her right, yanking everything into place again, and lurched into Ty Harkasian, who, being twenty-five, was vaulting up two steps at a time. He grabbed her before she completely lost her footing.

"Ty! God, I'm so sorry."

"That's okay, Lila. Are you all right? Careful on these stairs. They can be dangerous." His friendly smile almost completely masked his impatience to get to his classroom. He released her elbow and called a "Have a good day," over his shoulder as he raced on. Lila toiled onward to the next floor.

Not quite gasping, but making a vow to repeat yesterday's afternoon run at least twice a week, she arrived on the third floor. It was sheer vanity, but she tried not to sound out of breath as she called, "Good morning!" into 302 as she passed. Computer teacher and long-distance runner Mary Ann Himmelstein, looked up briefly from revving up her machines for the day. "Hi, Lila!"

Lila rounded the corner, coming suddenly upon an embracing couple nearly painted upon the tile walls. "Hey, you two. It's not even first period yet." They separated briefly, but probably only long enough for her to walk away.

With a "Hey, Bill," to her colleague in 304, she extricated her room key from the tangle of objects in her hand and unlocked her own door.

She still had ten minutes before class actually began but students had begun drifting in. Some were in her first period class, but several were kids who routinely stopped by to visit at the beginning of their day.

Doreen swiveled in wearing an outfit that could only have been applied with a compressor. She teetered on her three inch purple heels, dropped her gym clothes off in a corner for later, and flashed a luminous smile, "See you, Miss Wallace."

Gilberto Nieves approached, his entrance narrowly missing Doreen's exit, clutching a huge roll of cardboard.

"Do you have a rubber band, Miss?" Regardless of age or marital status, all female teachers were invariably addressed by the students as "Miss".

"What have you got there, Gilberto?"

"My science presentation – I was up mad late trying to get it finished in time."

Lila pulled open her desk drawer and began rooting around. "May I see it?" she asked, glancing up from the tangle of paper clips and rulers. Gilberto proudly flattened the project against his chest, momentarily disappearing behind it. A little smeared, but with noteworthy detail and a creative use of color, he had portrayed the stages of photosynthesis. "Wow, that looks great. Here, take these rubber bands, and you'd better get to class." Gilberto thanked her and wrestled his project out of the room.

Now the last of her first period class was entering, some shuffling quietly to their desks, others still wandering around the room with raucous laughter or appearing before her with urgent requests.

"Can I go to the bathroom?"

"Stella, you just got here. I swear I must write you a bathroom pass every day of the week. There were no bathrooms on your path from the front door to my room?"

"Please, Miss. It's an emergency. I don't feel so good."

The girl did look a little green around the gills. Ruminating that for the number of "emergencies" she was involved in each day, she should start calling herself an EMT, Lila quickly wrote a pass. She handed it to the student and started on attendance as the final bell rang. Some students rolled their eyes when relentlessly melodious tones of Anthony Paschetti emerged from the intercom over the door. He was easily the kids' least-liked of the administrators in the building. "Good morning. Today is Tuesday, September nineteenth, and students should now be in their "A" block class. Please stand for the Pledge of Allegiance."

The Pledge completed, Paschetti continued, embracing his daily spotlight, sounding uncannily like a flight attendant, with his careful pronunciation and singsong cadence. "Students are reminded that electronic devices of any description are forbidden on school grounds." Lila noticed one student looking quietly at her phone while another returned one to a friend two seats away. "Hats are not to be worn in the building." A group of three boys passed her door loudly, two of them with backwards New York Yankees baseball caps on their heads.

When Paschetti finally ended his monologue, it was time to get everyone focused. "Okay, folks, clear your desks of everything except a pen or pencil." Looks of horror washed across the room.

"Yo, Miss! A quiz?"

"Why didn't you tell us?"

"That's why it's called a *pop* quiz, Roberto. And from the looks of confidence I see, I can tell that everyone read last night's assignment." The class was unamused by her sarcasm. Marianne and Terrence put their heads on their desks while William tossed his pen down, folded his arms, and leaned back angrily in his chair. Others in the room showed their individual reactions less noticeably. Sasha smiled quietly to herself in her seat by the door, and Jacob and Warren on the other side of the room didn't seem particularly perturbed. Okay, thought Lila, at least someone read the play. She passed out half sheets of paper and said, "List five new things you learned about Macbeth in last night's assignment."

Sasha made a tidy stack of her facts and put down her pen while others in the room had mixed success in meeting the quota. Jacob, as usual, wrote quickly and messily; he still operated under the fiction that there would be a prize for whoever finished first. Warren took the opposite tack, going into long, torturous detail, turning his paper over for more room. The rest of the class either tried to save face by getting something, anything, on paper, or else dramatically wrote nothing, as if to underscore the unfairness of it all.

Lila gathered up the papers without comment, other than to say, "I now have ALL the quizzes, right? Anything that is turned in later will not be counted." She had been teaching long enough to outmaneuver someone who might try to slip in a paper after the answers had been discussed in class. Lila put the papers in the class folder, perched on the edge of her desk, and looked around the room. "So. Who's the bad guy? Macbeth or Lady Macbeth?" And they were off, even those with a tenuous grasp of the play determined to be heard.

***

The afternoon sun was warm on the shed door as it swung open easily to Sam's pull. A field mouse quickly scrabbled for a darker hideout during this intrusion. A glistening black mound of sunflower seeds lay beside the torn corner of a bag. It was surprisingly warm in the shed, warmer than the autumn air in the garden, which was growing cool in spite of the mid-afternoon sun. Sam reached for the clippers, dislodging several shovels and rakes; it had been a long time since he'd gotten in here to tidy up. It wasn't as though he didn't have time – he'd had nothing but time after May died. As he piled the tools back up he caught a glimpse of bright pink – not a color often seen among these grey and brown implements. He reached in and lifted from the dusty floor a crumpled straw hat, the brim with a few minute mouse nips and a deeply pink scarf tied around its crown.

His tall frame folded as he sank to the hood of his green riding mower. The metal emitted a small protest as it cupped under his weight. He held the hat in his calloused hands and stared dumbly at it. This belonged on May's short curls, not here, forgotten by all but the mice. Unbelievably, though it was years now since she'd died, the memory of her still had the power to slice right through him. But he also knew that he'd been alone too long, and there were days when he felt as overlooked by life as this hat. It would be good to see Lila this evening.

Sam smoothed the hat out gently, hung it on the nail inside the door and walked out with the clippers, closing the door carefully behind him.

\*\*\*

That evening, Lila knocked at the green screen door over the sounds of dishes and cutlery emanating from within. "Sam? You there?"

The old maple floor creaked at Sam's approach. He smiled down at her.

"Hey there, neighbor!"

He reached out to hold the door open as she entered, passing so closely that she could smell his clean scent of ordinary bath soap. The smells built, one upon the other, bath odors giving way tantalizingly to garlic and onion, fresh thyme and basil, all sautéing gently in olive oil in a cast iron skillet. The plain white wainscoting shone around the borders of the room, while a huge but tidy stack of newspapers sat near the door. A scrubbed wooden table was in the middle of the room, two old press-backed chairs were pulled up to it, their caned seats still in good repair. Sam stood, wooden spoon in hand, a bright red chef's apron protecting his blue flannel shirt. The shirt really deepened the blue in his eyes, Lila thought irrelevantly.

Later, after warming up with hummus and crisp red peppers, they had pretty much laid waste to the meal on the old pine kitchen table, neither one of them shy about having a good appetite. Slim legs stretched out before her in jeans, and her top half equally comfortable in an olive tank and plaid shirt, Lila buttered the last yeasty corner of a chunk of fresh whole wheat bread. Leafy autumn smells drifted in from the sides of the bay window and wove themselves into the ratatouille that still hung in the air.

"Where'd you get this bread, Sam? It's fabulous."

"Made it. I can knead dough with the best of them."

"Well, this is amazing. You've turned into quite the cook. Too bad it's all so good for you. I can't even feel a twinge of conscience."

"The joys of a vegan diet. Save room for my dairy-free rice pudding. I have some fresh peaches from Woods Farm. Josiah may be as old as the dirt in my field but his orchard still produces the best peaches around. How're things at school?"

"Oh I don't know, Sam. The same I guess - good kids, troubled kids, and downright awful kids. But as for the powers that be, I feel a change in the wind. I mean, speaking of older than dirt, Mr. Sweetwater's on his last year. Then we have Anthony Paschetti, who's only two months into his new role as VP and is strutting around puffed up with his own wonderfulness. And I don't think sitting in the principal's chair is doing Thelma Galaska any good. She always looks pale and tired these days. Our administration is fraying at the edges."

"Don't you have another assistant principal who's pretty capable?"

"Maritza Concepcion. She's really sharp, but she'll be out before November on maternity leave."

"Well, that's not so bad. I imagine the system will find someone to fill in while she's out."

"Maybe, but we're operating on some pretty shaky legs. Too bad we can't lure you into the city."

He cleared his throat, pushed back his chair and headed for the fridge. "I know this pudding will brighten your day. Reach behind you and get that bowl of peaches I cut up earlier."

He's really dodging that suggestion, thought Lila. Was his retirement permanent? She hoped not. Maybe what he needed to kick-start that newly-forgetful mind was to return to the career he'd been so good at. She placed the bright yellow bowl on the table as Sam turned with the pudding. Her eye and then her hand caught the container as it slipped from his grasp.

"Shoot! I must have forgotten to wipe off the outside of that." She noted that the exterior of the plastic storage tub was perfectly clean. Come to think of it, Sam's manipulation of the serving spoon had been awkward when he had served her earlier. Was it possible he was old enough for arthritis to be setting in?

"Here, why don't I serve us and you tell me what you've gleaned of town news while lounging around here when I'm in the big city sculpting young minds."

"Lounging???" Sam's left eyebrow shot much higher than she would have believed possible. "And this after wolfing down a meal created from ingredients produced by the sweat of my brow, you ungrateful person."

She smiled up from her pudding at his mock bluster.

He tapped the table as he spoke. "Well, let's see. I know people are getting pretty lathered up about taxes. The high school's been held together for too long with optimism and quick fixes. And where's the town going to find the revenue for a new one? We need the money that rolls in from commerce, but no one wants businesses to come and change the town."

"My, my. The inner-city halls of academe are looking calm in comparison." She stood up and took her dish to the sink. "I should probably pack it in, but first, how about I wash and you dry?"

"Nope, back off from that sink; there aren't enough to bother with. I'll get to them in the morning. If you must leave, let me walk you to the end of the drive."

They stepped out onto the porch and both stopped for a moment to breath in the evening. Soon this velvet warmth would turn crisp, and then cold. They descended the two steps and crunched down the gravel drive. A startled rabbit dived into a stand of grasses.

"Thanks, Sam, another great meal. I'll have to get you over to my place for a big dose of barbecue."

"Thank you for the offer, Li, but not unless you're grilling portabellas. No meat for me."

"Oh, I know, kidding, kidding. I just want to get some protein and vitamins into you along with all those vegetables."

"Vegetables are stacked with vitamins! I'm doing just fine. I only wish everyone would realize the benefits of a vegan diet. Mind you, it needs to be followed correctly – skip the doughnuts, French fries and corn chips. But done right, the rewards are healthier hearts and a reduced risk of cancer. And then there's the benefit to our planet as a whole – the efficiency of eating plants instead of feeding them to animals that will be slaughtered and consumed. Less land and water needed to feed more people!"

"I don't think I'm ready to convert just yet - I'd miss the culinary magic of a good steak too much." She pulled her flashlight from her pocket. "Well, good night neighbor. Thanks for a wonderful meal."

"It was my pleasure." He stood smiling in his driveway, watching her as she walked away.

Not needing the flashlight to see her way on this starry night, she instead kept it trained on the ground near her feet to alert any cars that might be traveling down the quiet road,. She could hear the last of the peepers screaming at each other in a nearby boggy field. A late dove or early owl called as something scurried around in the roadside weeds. This was her absolute favorite moment – a warm fall evening. She was actually happy to enjoy it alone without having it interrupted by conversation. She told herself it was just as well that Craig was gone.

Still, at times her old farmhouse still seemed to resonate with the memory of Craig's quick footsteps as he would charge off to his next project. But selling suburban houses in a bedroom community didn't have quite the same kick as turning over million dollar properties to diplomatic attachés in Washington.

Yeah, right, Lila, she told herself. As though the tribulations of a shaky market had been the real reason for his departure.

Maybe another factor had also been that she had realized he was not the man for the life she was beginning to see for herself. Growing up, she'd been the cliché of the small town girl who couldn't wait to leave. She'd been thrilled after graduating from college to be hired by that small D.C. newspaper. Even after it folded she had loved the area enough to begin a career as a teacher in the challenging city schools. But now that she'd returned to Calvin she remembered the feel of land she'd walked as a child, the shorthand of talking with people who'd known her forever.

Her toe grazed a rutabaga-sized rock that had been freed from the bordering stone wall by time or an industrious chipmunk. As she regained her balance she glanced ahead to see a small foreign sports car pull into the Wetherill's drive. It didn't reappear, so it wasn't an off-course driver looking for a place to turn around. Perhaps the new owner? She yawned and continued toward her own house. One set of tests to grade, lunch to make for tomorrow and then maybe she could stay awake long enough to get through a chapter of her latest murder mystery. Her evening looked full enough without worrying about the new neighbor. She'd probably run into him – or her – soon enough.

# CHAPTER FOUR

Lila's morning had progressed pretty well. A surprising number of the kids had actually done last night's homework and one class had enjoyed some lively debate on the reading, buoyed by the exotically unfamiliar experience of genuine knowledge of the material.

Her second period class ended and she stayed at her desk for a few moments as the students filed out. Getting her handouts and assignments organized before the next class could often mean the difference between a smooth lesson and an unproductive one.

A "Mmmhmm!" from her doorway caused her to look up. Anthony Paschetti stood there, a disapproving look on his face.

"Yes, Mr. Paschetti?"

"I hope you plan to join the rest of us here in the hall, Miss Wallace. You know school policy – we need teachers to help ensure orderly passage in between classes."

Lila sighed. She was one of the more faithful when it came to overseeing the hallways. How maddening to be called out this one time by Paschetti, of all people.

"Of course, Mr. Paschetti. I was on my way." She stacked up one last pile and stood up as Paschetti strutted out triumphantly. When she reached her door she saw him hurry away to avoid confronting two hefty basketball stars competing to touch the exit sign bolted high at the end of the hall. Instead, he broke up a giggling group of tiny freshman girls who were standing quietly to the side.

The elevator door mid-way down the hall opened, emitting Principal Galaska and Maritza Concepcion. They looked to be on their way to Concepcion's office. No wonder they took the elevator, thought Lila. Maritza looked to be on the verge of her maternity leave, but of the two, Galaska looked more in need of some time away from the stresses of running a high school. The principal's face seemed paler than usual; the assistant principal, as pregnant as she was, had more spring in her step. Lila glanced away and realized that Paschetti had paused in the hall and was watching them intently, a scowl on his face.

Third period, Lila herded her class into their seats in the auditorium, no easy task, since like maverick calves wandering away from the herd, several kids hoped to escape her eye long enough to sit with their friends. She cut Terrance off at the pass – or at least the aisle – and directed him to a seat. "There you go, Terrance. I've picked out a comfortable seat just for you next to me. Aren't you lucky?" He folded his long legs and sat with a gloomy sideways glance at her. She reached to the row in front to pull William's baseball cap off of his head and tapped Marianne on the shoulder when she started to pull her phone from her purse.

The auditorium was just about full, the senior class settling in beneath banners representing past graduating classes. Jerome Sweetwater and Maritza Concepcion were strategically positioned at the front corners, lasering quelling stares at the noisier sections of the hall. It was good they were both able to summon effective auras of authority. Neither the aging black man nor the visibly pregnant young woman was exactly a tower of physical strength. She wondered briefly why Paschetti, the only able-bodied member of the administrative team, was absent, but then he had already proven himself adept in side-stepping the more onerous administrative tasks, particularly ones that involved confrontations with students over five feet tall.

Principal Galaska slowly climbed the steps onto the stage, followed by the senior class advisor, Maura Mary O'Shaughnessy, who was known to all staff, and probably many of the students, as M&M. Mrs. Galaska stepped to the mike attached to the lectern. "Good morning, seniors!" Only September, this was new status for most, so this was met with an excited roar of "Good morning!" More threatening rays from the two assistant principals, supported by teachers, and the room calmed.

"This is an exciting time for you. You will face many challenges in the coming year, with grades and college applications. It is also a year with some financial obligations. Obligations such as yearbooks, class rings, the class trip, and senior prom." Mrs. Galaska seemed to grasp the edge of the lectern more tightly and paused to take a big breath. In the third row, Lila looked up at her sharply, wondering if she was caught by emotion or if in fact, the principal was actually unwell. However, Galaska continued in a strong voice. "Since few of us can claim to be independently wealthy" – laughter, cat-calling, searing administrative stares and two of the more boisterous hauled out of the auditorium by teachers – "we plan to have several fund raisers to help you participate in this year's activities. Here to explain our fall event is Miss O'Shaughnessy."

Enthusiastic applause broke out as Miss O'Shaughnessy took Mrs. Galaska's place at the microphone. At an attractive thirty-three, and shorter than many of those in the class, M&M was a compassionate special education teacher who worked the kids hard but was respected throughout the school.

Mrs. Galaska stepped off the stage, assisted on the last step by Mr. Sweetwater, who held her elbow and spoke to her for a moment. Mrs. Galaska shook her head and pulled her elbow away, steadying herself on the edge of the stage. She patted her grey curls, straightened her tweed suit jacket and left by the side entrance.

Later that morning, Lila decided it would be a good time to drop off outside work for two of her students who had been suspended from school. With over fifteen years of teaching she knew better than to send home anything such as precious class room texts she might actually want to see again. Nevertheless, she was able to assemble two hefty packets of assignments that would keep the missing scholars up to speed with events in class.

Carrying the folders, she locked her door and turned, only to see Anthony Paschetti berating a teary-faced girl a few yards down the hall near the school's elevator. Passing students looked over as they went by, but kept a safe distance from the angry administrator and the sniffling girl, who Lila recognized as a Sasha, one of her best students.

Lila walked over, "What seems to be the matter, Mr. Paschetti?"

"Ms. Wallace. I am explaining to this young lady that the elevator is not for the use of students unless they have been given a key by the main office. Our friend here seems to think it was installed for the sole purpose of providing joy-rides." He stepped menacingly toward the diminutive girl, whose head barely reached Lila's shoulder.

"My goodness, I find that surprising. This doesn't sound like Sasha at all. Sasha, what do you have to say for yourself?"

In a voice that was barely audible, the girl said, "I was helping Brittany."

"And whoever this Brittany is, and whether she needs your help, which I doubt, this does not give you leave to ride the elevator for your amusement. I believe Mr. Bookman in the in-house suspension room will be happy to provide you with a seat." Paschetti's mouth curled in a sarcastic smile as he spoke.

Lila put her hand on the girl's shoulder. "Sasha? What do you mean you were helping Brittany?"

Sasha looked up at Lila, tears wet on her cheeks. In one breath, she said, "Brittany is on crutches so she can't use the stairs and she *has* an elevator key, I swear, and she couldn't carry her books so I told the nurse I'd help her and then when it stopped on this floor her boyfriend came and got the books and she left and I was getting off when Mr. Paschetti came up and –" Her gulping at the point precluded any more explanation.

Lila turned to the assistant principal. "There, I guess we've straightened that out, haven't we, Mr. Paschetti? Sasha, why don't you go to the girls' room and wash your face and then get to class?"

After hesitating for a moment and casting a frightened look at the assistant principal, Sasha hurried away, worried that her reprieve might be rescinded. Paschetti's mouth seemed to be opening and closing - not unlike a cod, thought Lila, looking at the thwarted bully - but he gained control and compressed his lips into a thin line of annoyance. "Well, Ms. Wallace, it looks as though that young . . .lady has you to thank for her undeserved liberation. I just hope she won't now continue to think she can play fast and loose with the school rules."

Lila smiled sweetly, "I guess that's just the chance we'll have to take," and left before she gave in to her first impulse, which was to kick this petty tyrant in the shin.

She weaved and dodged through the chaotic hallway as the late bell rang for class. Just like the five other times it rang each day, it had practically no effect. The couple locked in an embrace stayed clinched, the two girls near her continued to shriek happily to each other, and the three young men by the double doors carried on using the frame to do chin-ups, blocking anyone hoping to pass through and actually get to class.

Muttering to herself about deafness in today's youth, she opened the door to the main office. The decibel level dropped noticeably, although somehow the air still felt as full of emotion. Sorting mail, Tiana Weeks, the ageless Jamaican school head secretary, without whom the whole place would disintegrate, deftly fielded a parent's question while directing history teacher Bill Lemur to where the field trip forms were stored. Her two assistants at their desks alternately answered phones and glanced nervously down the short inner hall to the principal's office.

Kashana Sullivan and Joyce Ronley, who, like Lila, were on their class-free planning period, stood to the side looking worried. Lila joined them by the wooden files for in and out-going mail and said, "What's going on?"

Kashana said, "Not sure, but Thelma's not doing so good - been looking sketchy since this morning."

Lila said, "You know, I thought she looked pretty unsteady at the assembly earlier. She almost needed help getting off the stage."

Moving a stack of books so that she could lean against the low counter more comfortably, Joyce folded her arms and said, "I wonder if it had anything to do with Paschetti's visit to her earlier today."

Kashana and Lila turned to her. "Why?" asked Lila. "What would that have to do with anything?"

Joyce lowered her voice, "All I know is she called him in to her office. I heard there'd been some complaint about him from a parent -"

"Mmm hmm," nodded Kashana. "Ain't no surprise there."

"Well, afterwards he came out smiling that nasty smile of his and Thelma asked Tiana to hold her calls, she didn't want to be disturbed, and I heard she looked really upset."

"Maybe that rumor about him having something on her isn't such a rumor after all," mused Lila.

At this moment the door to the main office swung open and Ty Harkasian entered quickly with the school nurse in tow, and rushed past them to the principal's office. When the three women glanced down the hall they could see Thelma behind her desk looking drained and oddly smaller as the nurse bent over her. The nurse turned around suddenly and called over her shoulder, "Tiana, get an ambulance here, fast."

# CHAPTER FIVE

It was Friday, but it was too early for much of a crowd in O'Brannan's except for the staff from the high school just up the street. Lila waited for her usual Black and Tan, and then, beer in hand, traveled past the empty tables to Kashana, Joyce, and Ty.

Kashana looked up and smiled, her gold hoops shining beneath her trim Afro, "What a day! Hi, Lila. Wish I could have one of those – I could do with a little Bass and Guinness about now, but this Coke is gonna have to be it. I've got to pick up the kids and get Trevaughn to his soccer game. At least I have my trusty lawn chair. Standing on the sidelines after six hours of teaching isn't my idea of a good time. You left school last, Lila. Any word on Thelma?"

"Nope, none."

Ty was momentarily distracted by the arrival of the evening bartender, all blond hair and cleavage, but turned back to ask, "They called Mr. Sweetwater to cover the rest of the day, didn't they?"

Joyce was on the far end of her forties and finishing up divorce number two and still radiated a lush sex appeal of her own. She noted Ty's glance with a latent sense of competition as she straightened the necklace that disappeared into the generous valley of her chest. "Yeah, poor Jerome was dropped feet first into Thelma's day – in spite of Paschetti's campaigning to get the job himself."

"Oh sure," said Ty. "Like anyone would even consider him."

"All I know is my source in Central Office said he was emailing everyone there with a pulse."

"The nerve of that guy. With his ego, you know he's gotta be mad he didn't get called to replace her." said Kashana.

"Anyway, Tiana said Jerome did pretty well – he met with that crazy Mrs. Dunleavy who was all worked up over a fracas on her son's school bus, which he probably caused, by the way. He also had to jump in between McKormick and Rogers on whether the library would be used for the medical careers fair next week or the kids' research for their AP history class. To top off the afternoon, he had to send Sean Pelletier home; he was caught stealing in the locker room."

Lila said, "Damn – I'll have to see who won the library. I thought I'd bring my honors class there for some work on the computers. And I did pop my head in the office before I left. Jerome looked worn out. He told me he had no interest in a repeat performance and that it was no wonder Thelma had left on a stretcher."

Kashana, with her face in her voluminous brown purse, placed hand wipes, one athletic sock, a baggie of raisins, and two trucks – one aqua, the other red – on the table. Finally raising her car keys in victory, she said, "Well I gotta go. Have one for me."

Sweeping everything back into her purse, she pushed back her chair. "And you know we all love Mr. Sweetwater. He's a good man, he's been there forever, but it's his last year. Ain't no one with any sense gonna take over a school like ours when he's sixty-five, with eight months to retirement." Her phone rang as she left the table. She pulled it successfully from her bag on the first try. "Yeah, honey, I'm on my way. Get your cleats on and I'll be there in ten minutes. . ." and she was out of the door.

Lila turned to Joyce, "So where does that leave us? Thelma won't be back any time soon. We don't have much to pick from for her replacement."

Joyce shifted in her chair, releasing a small "whooph" of patchouli. "You're not kidding. The talent pool is getting pretty shallow."

Lila said, "Without Mr. Sweetwater that leaves either Maritza Concepcion or Tony Paschetti."

"Yeah, it's not looking too good," said Joyce. "Tony's a product of that 90-day wonder program for new administrators and besides being really bad with kids, doesn't know his ass from his elbow. Never mind that we all think he only got the job through shady dealings. And we can't pin our hopes on Maritza. She's as sharp as a new protractor, but she'll only be around till November. Plus, have you seen the size of her lately? She's getting so big with that baby I don't know how she fits behind her desk."

"What a way to begin the year." Ty held up his empty beer glass. "That calls for another."

"Not me. I'm heading for home. You and Joyce have a good weekend."

"Wait up, Lila. I'll walk you out." She turned to Ty, "And now you'll be able to chat up that cute thing behind the bar without us around to slow you down." Joyce laughed warmly as he flushed.

He rose from his chair and helped them gather their things. "Nope, not my type. Sorry to see you go, ladies." He smiled deeply at them, the curls in his hair almost blue in the dim bar.

Lila and Joyce pushed out into the sunlight.

"Drinking at 4:30! This is what teaching will do to a person." Joyce pulled out her sunglasses.

"I think it's coming out of a bar into the blazing sun that makes it feel so wicked. Good thing our transgressions are cancelled out by all the young lives we've turned around this week."

"Yeah, right, Lila. Speak for yourself. I'm still just trying to get my classes to stay in their seats long enough so I can take attendance."

"Now that's not true. I happen to know that your students are better prepared than any other science teacher's at the end of the year."

"Well, I don't know about that, but they haven't blown anything up this week, so that's a good thing."

"Absolutely. Where did you park?"

"I'm up the street. I'll see you on Monday. Let's hope next week is better."

Lila waved and turned the corner to the lot next to the bar.

Just leaving her car was Margaret Daniele, the assistant superintendent in charge of the city's high schools. Margaret had been an upwardly mobile assistant principal when Lila had returned to the area three years ago. She and Lila had been friendly when they worked together, but she had never revealed to Lila whether she regretted her move into the often political climate at the school department's Central Office. She must not have had too bad a day if it had ended so early.

"Lila! What a nice surprise! It's been too long – we need to get together for dinner soon."

"Margaret, it's so good to see you. You remind me of the good old days of teaching."

"Oh come on, it wasn't that long ago and it wasn't any better – you were just a little younger and less jaded." Margaret smiled in her tailored suit of harvest colors that was a perfect match for her short auburn hair.

"You're right about that, but it's still been a hell of a week. Thelma Galaska had a heart attack at school today."

"Oh my God, that's awful! I had no idea – I've been stuck in budget meetings all day. How is she? If I'm right, this isn't her first."

"We don't have any real news, but she'll be in the hospital at least through the weekend, and then she's sure to need some convalescent time."

"I'll have to get there and pay her a visit. You know, she and I taught together back when dinosaurs roamed the earth."

"No, I knew she had begun as a history teacher, but I didn't know you had worked together."

Margaret spun her sunglasses in her hand as she thought back. "Yes, we were across the hall from each other for five years. She wasn't the toughest teacher in the world, but she was fair to the kids. I wish more teachers realized the importance of teaching by the golden rule."

"That's pretty much how she's run the school, too. But now I don't know where we are or who's going to fill in while she's out. There are several reasons why I don't think any of our VPs are up to the task."

Margaret leaned against her car and listened attentively as Lila recounted the weaknesses of the administrative staff at Thomas Paine. She noticed Margaret didn't look particularly surprised by her summation of Paschetti's failings.

Margaret glanced over as a car pulled into the lot. "Lila, my sister's here. I'll give this some thought. This is bad timing since we just finished staffing all the schools. We really don't have anyone to spare."

"Well, as you're ruminating this weekend, I do have a wild card to throw into the mix – Sam Fielding."

"The principal at Calvin High? I thought he retired."

"He did. When his wife was ill. But she passed away a few years ago and I think he could be persuaded to fill in. I'm so glad I ran into you, Margaret. I hope you can help us out of this snarl we're in."

The two friends exchanged hugs and parted as a woman with the same shade of hair and brisk demeanor as Margaret's emerged smiling from her car. Lila hoped her suggestion would be taken seriously. Getting Sam to Thomas Paine High might fix two problems at the same time, repairing both a shaky infrastructure at her school and Sam's absentmindedness.

# CHAPTER SIX

Lila sat on the floor of her bedroom Saturday morning with a half-finished mug of coffee at her side and pulled the cardboard box out from under her bed. Four CDs, one pair of leather flip-flops, *Real Estate, the Key to Your Future*, a baseball cap, and photographs of a handsome couple at a variety of venues in a variety of poses. Craig and Lila, Lila and Craig, Craig, Lila, Craig.

He was a city boy when they had first met in front of that Van Gogh in the National Gallery. Her childhood had been punctuated by tree forts, apple wars, and twilight football with neighborhood kids. His had been made up of city streets and basketball on asphalt under street lamps. That day he had been in between house closings in Georgetown; she'd been in Washington for a textbook convention. She thought about that evening together weeks later in Arlington, when she had told him about growing up here in Calvin. It was not a candlelight and roses date; instead it had held the ease grown from many dates: sock feet and pizza.

"- so in this epic neighborhood apple war, why didn't you use peaches instead of apples?" Craig had asked.

"The apples made a better sound when they hit our trash can lid shields. Plus, we could get away with wasting apples at the Sullivans'. My parents would have skinned me alive if I'd used our peaches."

"You must have made a pretty good target," Craig had laughed and reached to pluck an errant green pepper off of her chin.

"I wasn't always this tall, plus it's easier to find a tree to duck behind when you're skinny."

His response could have held a warning, if only she had listened more closely: "Never mind your idyllic childhood stories. I'm glad I had sidewalks and bus fumes. Give me an all-night newspaper stand and Chinese restaurants where I can track down the perfect egg roll."

A city boy he had remained. After he had joined her in Calvin, sitting with him on the porch some evenings she had imagined she could hear his inner engine revving at high idle, impatient with the slow pace of the town. That last day he had shrugged, smiled that fatal smile, and confessed the country was too long on quiet and too short on excitement. But they both knew this was only part of the story; even during their time together in Washington she'd never been willing to talk about staying together permanently, let alone marrying him.

And how did she feel about all this now? Lila held the faded Yankees baseball cap to her chest and considered this. She wasn't exactly pining away. She'd had the summer to re-accustom herself to solitary living, and on reflection she decided she was just fine. It did take some adjustment – when Craig moved in, her friendship with Margaret Daniele was not the only one she had allowed to drop away. Now, not only was there no Craig, but her social life was limited to the hours between 7 am and 4 pm at school.

It was the idea of him that she missed more that his actual corporal being. And the box – this last vestige of him – could go as well. She tossed the hat back in with the other mementoes and stood up. Juggling the box and mug, she went downstairs and out to her car where she put the box in the trunk, along with everything else that was on its last roundup to the town dump.

She arrived at the recycling center, where the Saturday trash square dance, accompanied by polka music piped from the DPW's shack, was in full swing. Town residents too thrifty to pay for private garbage pick-up passed from late-model sedans to paper masher, from sagging trucks to the Boy Scout bottle donation area, or do-si-doed from the giant can and plastic bin over to the glass collection zone. Some nodded a generic hello as they passed, others spotted neighbors and stopped mid-stride to trade news, recyclables in hand.

Calvin had recently graduated to blazing pink bags with the town emblem. They barely contained a standard black trash bag, and at two dollars each, townies employed a variety of creative tactics to fit as much as possible in them. Last Saturday Lila had watched a woman in a fetching outfit of too-short sweat pants, socks, felt clogs and what appeared to be her son's team jacket, pull a bag from the trunk of her silver BMW. It was the regulation pink bag, but it was trying valiantly to contain a larger black bag intended for a 55 gallon trash bin. Good thing she'd had a second pink bag with her since she'd never made it past the dump despot, a veteran town employee with the cold eyes of someone who's seen it all.

Lila tossed her own pink offering into the maws of the giant compacter, tipped her cans into the bin, and walked some books over to the donation area. As she was shutting her trunk she glanced across at the giant silver SUV next to her. Some very broad shoulders were emerging from the driver's seat. Really, she thought. Could that vehicle be any more obnoxious? Unless this man with the impossibly curly dark blonde hair and broad smile had a need to storm across country dodging antelope while simultaneously listening to surround-sound, why would anyone need such a vehicle? He caught her eye and she ducked into her car. She didn't remember having seen him around town before - good thing, too. Honestly! People who felt the need for such an egregious display must be flawed in some way. Although judging by what she'd seen so far, the flaws were certainly not physical ones. The polka music played on and the plastic sunflowers nailed to the shack dipped in the sun as she left the dump.

Next came the post office where she needed to sign for and then mail off a registered letter for the long-gone Craig. Must be some tax documents following him around. She hoped she'd be able to sign for him. How awkward for both of them if he had to trek back to Calvin to pick them up. A good omen – the parallel parking in front of the post office offered two empty spots, which meant she could pull right in without employing any advanced parking skills. She turned to unearth the registered letter notice tossed onto the back seat and a shaft of silver lasered through her rear window, momentarily blinding her. The morning light in her car darkened as a rolling behemoth pulled in behind.

Still frozen in her reach, she watched as a not-quite-burly but very solid form bounded athletically into the building. Was the man everywhere? She slammed her door and noted the huge chrome-encased grill enveloping the front of his vehicle. She wondered what possible purpose it could have.

Repelling stray water buffaloes?

A typical Saturday at the post office – the line of customers was five deep. And of course there he was, last in line. She took her place in back of him, and noticed with a petty flash of superiority that he was only about an inch taller. Her mind wandered slightly as she contemplated his muscular, tanned neck, framed with blond curls. They drew adjacent tellers, he stood before a woman who smiled and smoothed her hair as she waited on him. Lila got Ben Coskey, a face familiar to her ever since they had shared a crayon tub in Mrs. Chabot's kindergarten class. Ben's receding chin, only a possibility at five, had in adulthood become a fact. "Hey, Lila, good to see you. You okay out there in your parent's place?"

"I'm just fine, Ben. It's a comfortable old house, although now that it's mine I'm noticing it could use a little work. Somehow when you're a kid you don't see the trees growing out of the gutters or the loose floorboard. I'm wondering – can you help me with this? I have some registered mail that I need to redirect -"

"Oh, sure. Where's this going? D.C.? No problem."

As Ben sorted forms, stapling and rubber-stamping, Lila listened to the conversation to her left.

"78 Old County Road? You're in the old Wetherill place. Welcome to Calvin,

Mr. -" The teller paused as she attempted to read the name on the mail-forwarding slip.

A hearty laugh rose over the general chatter. "Athanasopoulos. Looks like you'll just have to call me Niko, Cynthia." His muscled forearm rested on the counter as he leaned in, smiling; he had apparently noted the name tag sitting just above her left breast. Cynthia's face flushed slightly as he took his mail and then saluted her with it slightly as he exited. The teller seemed mesmerized for a moment by the now-empty doorway, her mouth still open, a hand resting on the base of her throat.

\*\*\*

It may have only been the two of them, but the gate-leg table on Sam's porch was awash with food. Lila leaned back, the last bite of deep-dish vegetable pie on the blue willow plate (her second helping) an unattainable goal.

"Are you sure you wouldn't like more of these cucumbers in vinegar? I think the fresh dill and touch of sugar make all the difference."

"Sam, why don't you weigh 300 pounds? This homemade pie crust alone just cancelled all of my last week's salads."

"Well, the potatoes, carrots, bok choy, and cauliflower in that pie didn't plant and pick themselves. And nothing but good can come of vegetables; they give us what we need but take nothing from any other living thing."

Sam sat silent for a moment, rearranging the salt and pepper shakers in front of him. In the shape of nesting tomatoes, they were evidence of his wife May's fondness for quirky kitchenware. As he picked one up, it fell from his grasp and dropped to the table, chipping a green ceramic leaf.

"Well, now, shoot! I'm getting too clumsy for my own good. What do you say we take our iced tea down there to the end of the porch?"

"Let me just help you get these dishes to the kitchen."

"No, leave them be, Lila. They'll be fine. I've got some news that might interest you."

As they pushed away from the table and then stood, Sam grasped the back of his chair quickly and seemed to sway for a beat. But then Lila thought that perhaps she had been wrong; it had been nothing. He picked up his glass and with a courtly gesture, waved Lila to the green wicker chairs filled with bright chintz pillows. They settled themselves amid the creakings of the old woven reeds and put their glasses on the steamer trunk that served as a coffee table. The daylight in the yard was dimming, infusing everything with a soft rosy glow, and there were occasional flashes outside the screen from the last of the summer fireflies.

Lila sighed in contentment and then, forcing herself into a more upright position, said, "So what's up, Sam? What's your news?"

Was that an excited gleam in his eye? "Well, let's just say that it's a good thing the growing season is drawing to a close. It looks like I'm not going to have much time for working out in the garden. Although how I'll get my fall canning done. . . ."

"Why? What do you mean?"

"How would you like some company on the ride into school on Monday?"

"Oh Sam! Are you going to be filling in for Thelma? That's fabulous, although I wonder if you'll think so after a couple of days at TP."

"TP?"

"Oh, sorry. That's what the kids call it, and I guess I picked it up from them – Thomas Paine. Boy, can we use you. The beginning of the year is tough enough without playing musical chairs in the head office. Once the kids feel like we're not all on the same page, it's an ugly slide downhill for the rest of the year. We can definitely use someone who can keep the school on track."

"Well, I'll do the best I can. I'm a little rusty, it's been almost three years now."

"Oh, please. Enough with the false modesty. You've forgotten more about leading a school than some people ever learn in a lifetime." She mentally smacked herself on the forehead. Probably not the best choice of words. His memory had been on the skids a bit lately. Fortunately, her comments appeared to have gone past without notice.

"So I'd better earn my keep as a passenger. Time for a dish of peach crumble. I know you like it with gingersnaps all broken up on top."

"Oh my god, Sam. You may have to drive on Monday after all. I'll be too fat to fit behind the steering wheel."

"You take after your Dad with your height, Lila. You have a long stretch of real estate to fill before you even get in the neighborhood of plump. I'll be right back with a big bowl of heaven."

She had known Sam off and on for so many years it was impossible to imagine he was flirting with her. He and May had moved to Calvin a few years before she left for college, and one or the other had often dropped by during her later visits home. As a married couple they had had more in common with her parents than with her and so she had always vaguely classified him as of an older generation. But watching him stride out of the room in search of dessert, she once again realized that he was really much closer to her age than theirs.

She had doubted if he was even aware of her presence when she came home from Virginia for May's funeral. Probably the only things holding him together at the time were his innate courtesy and the military grounding that had forced him to forge ahead through each step of the ceremony of death demanded by society.

Lila's parents had died soon after, one death closely following the other. Even in death, as in life, her parents were tied inextricably to each other, often to the exclusion of others. She had left her teaching position to deal with her duties as executor and Sam had been such a help with the legal and financial tangle they had left behind. Stereotypical as it was, as a college professor and a jewelry designer, both absorbed in their work, neither had strong record-keeping skills. It was amazing that there were any records at all. It was when he was helping her at that time that she first began to feel more like his contemporary, and soon they would apparently be colleagues, or more accurately, administrator and teacher.

She looked up from her musings to see him in the doorway, looking sheepish, red-checked dishtowel in hand.

"I was halfway through the pots when I realized I came in for the dessert. Can I get you anything to go with it? Coffee?"

"Nope, I'll take my calories straight up. But why don't I help you finish those dishes and work off some of that dinner before we dive into dessert?"

They gathered their dishes from the porch, carrying them into the kitchen. Sam already had a sink ready full of sudsy water. He returned to his task of washing and Lila reached up to pull the dish towel from his shoulder.

"So how's this vegan diet treating you, Sam? You've been on it for a while – you feeling okay?"

Surprised, he glanced over at her, his arms covered in suds. "Of course. I'm fine. And what could be better? I'm virtually self-sufficient since I raise practically everything I eat. Plus keeping my fields going is better than any trip to the gym." He handed her a plate to dry. She had to admit that he looked the picture of health – upright and lean, the well-defined muscles on his long arms flexing as he fished around in the sink for the next dish. He smiled at her, "Don't forget that the universal rules of dishwashing state that the wiper has to take care of anything the washer misses!"

Lila's answering smile dimmed when the plate he handed her slipped from his grasp. She caught it before it hit the slate countertop. Sam dismissed it by saying, "That one must have been a bit soapy."

# CHAPTER SEVEN

Sunday had begun with the paper, coffee, and the leftover peach crumble Sam had pressed upon her Saturday night. But okay, she hadn't exactly fought back with any conviction.

By mid-morning Lila worked up the energy to put on jeans and an old flannel shirt of Craig's for a foray to the Sisyphean mountain of cardboard boxes in the basement. How in the world had her parents accumulated so much when as a child it seemed as though the only things that claimed their interest were either in her father's study or her mother's studio? She had a feeling that before long she would cave and just cart everything, unseen, to the landfill or Salvation Army. Yet clearing all this out would bring her that much closer to whatever her new life in Calvin would be.

After a morning filled with dust and mildew she emerged sneezing into the daylight, only to remember that her freedom was short-lived. She still had two classes worth of essays to grade before Monday. She made a mental note to incorporate a bit more fun into this terrific new life she was shaping. The best way for anyone to learn to write well was through constant practice but unfortunately, that meant someone else had to grade that writing and provide feedback, even if it was received with blank stares and stuffed unread into never-emptied backpacks.

Hours later, ink-stained and shoulders aching, she finally was able to toss together a salad with some deli roast beef for her supper and take it and a nice fat roll outside to eat on the old flagstone patio. She lowered herself and the plate onto the faded cushions of the chaise lounge and glanced up to observe the last vestige of Winston disappearing through the screen door. She took a tired bite of the crusty roll. She told herself that she really needed to check the spring that held the door to the frame. Without a tight fit, insects could find their way in, looking for that last bit of summer warmth. And maybe field mice, coming in for the winter - -

She speared roast beef and romaine and replayed the past couple of minutes in her mind. An ominous suspicion crept into her thoughts. She knew from hard experience that the patter of tiny feet did not always have the power to gladden the heart. She heaved herself up and crossed the patio to the house.

The kitchen appeared benign: tea kettle on the stove, salad ingredients sat on the counter waiting to go back to the fridge. She passed through to the dining room – quiet. Hall - quiet. Living room – Winston. Or at least half of Winston, since the remainder of him appeared to be stuck under the old brocade couch, the skirt of the couch draped across his latter half. To judge by the movements of his tail, quite a bit seemed to be happening under there. And sure enough, from the other side she saw a streak of pale brown fur torpedo across the room to the hall and up the stairs, closely followed by the cat. After a few more rounds through the ten-room house – how much simpler it would be to live in a one-bedroom ranch – she managed to slap a laundry basket over cat and rabbit together and cha-cha'd both of them out the front door. She went back to gather up her dishes, eating the rest of her meal on her way to the sink. Winston and the rabbit would have to work out their issues on their own – outside.

\*\*\*

Now here it was Monday morning, the coming chill of autumn easy to spot at this hour. She pulled into Sam's drive, the crunch of her tires on the gravel loud in the early stillness. Waiting for him to emerge from the house, she sat in a mild stupor, still not fully awake, regardless of the giant mug of tea she'd polished off. She glanced up, her mental fog evaporating as Sam appeared, somehow taller, and definitely more handsome, in a gray suit and blindingly white shirt. He tossed his briefcase in the back, "Nothing much in that now except my lunch, but I bet it'll be full this afternoon." When he sat and turned to her she noticed the threads of blue in his jacket picked up the color of his eyes.

Get a grip, she thought. It's just Sam. Before she put the car into reverse, she waved her cell phone. "So, before we go, should I take a picture of you on your first day of school?"

"Better not jinx it – let's hope it's not my last."

"Sam, your reputation precedes you; when the staff learns you're filling in, you'll probably be greeted with rose petals strewn in your path."

"Well, hopefully Ms. Galaska will recover quickly and I won't be there long enough to do any lasting damage. But it's exciting to think about getting behind a desk again and seeing what I can do to help." How typical of Sam, she thought. No ego, and his only agenda is to lend a hand to someone else.

Before leaving his drive and turning toward town, she glanced to the left at the property abutting his. It looked as though someone was beginning to install new posts for a split-rail fence.

"Oh, gosh. That reminds me. I think I've seen your new neighbor. In fact, I can't seem to avoid him lately, him or his stupid leviathan of a car. His name is Niko something."

" Athanasopoulos. Seems like a good guy. Stopped by in his car as I was getting the mail out of the mailbox a couple of days ago. But I would definitely not label his car as a leviathan. It was an expensive little foreign job. If anything, it's almost too small for someone of his size."

"The guy I'm thinking of is pretty big, but I've seen him in some enormous suburban assault vehicle. Of course! It figures that he would have two cars, both obscenely expensive."

"Gosh, Lila. That's a lot of opinion for someone you haven't even met yet."

"Mmmmf," she snorted to herself. Obviously Sam was too nice to see this guy for the self-satisfied model of conspicuous consumption that he really was.

They drove out of Calvin in companionable silence. It felt right to be together on their way into work, as if they'd done this for years. They were both deep in their own thoughts, thoughts that changed with the geography from town to city. Any concerns of their private lives fell away as the professional ones drew physically closer.

She turned into the small parking area in the back of the school, saw an opening at the end of the row and pulled into it. Still a pretty good spot; she had managed to arrive in the first wave of teachers. With occasional curious glances from the few people in the almost-empty halls, Lila and Sam made their way to the main office.

Her shirt the vibrant shade of a ripe mango, Tiana looked up from her stack of mail and then hurried forward with a wide smile.

"Mr. Fielding it is! Cho! I have not even yet made room for you at Mrs. Galaska's desk! But welcome, welcome!" Her island accent thickened in her excitement. Hardly waiting for acknowledgement of her greeting, Tiana turned and scurried down the inner hall to the principal's office. Sam went through the large counter's swinging half door to follow the head secretary and Lila called after him, "You're obviously in good hands. I'll see you later. Have fun!" Sam waved over his shoulder at her as he followed Tiana.

Lila's day was punctuated by unmotivated students recovering from Monday-morning doldrums and curious teachers eager to extract information from her about Sam. She only wished the kids in her classes had a comparable thirst for knowledge. At last the end of the day finally arrived, and with it a faculty meeting, the teachers drifting in after straightening their rooms, helping that last student with a question, or running last minute copies critical for the next day. Everyone settled in the creaking auditorium chairs, and Jerome Sweetwater walked slowly to the lectern in front, his half-lens reading glasses perched on the end of his nose.

"I want to thank y'all for putting aside your busy lives for a bit and staying after school today. As you know, we had some unhappy business on Friday but Mrs. Galaska is in the hospital, resting comfortably and doing just fine. I've been told that she had a mild heart attack — now there's an oxymoron for you -," he paused for quiet laughter, "but the doctors would like to keep her under observation for a few days."

Kashana Sullivan's hand shot up. "So when will she be back, Jerome?"

"Well, now Kashana, we don't know that yet, but thank you for providing me with the perfect segue. The purpose of this gathering is to introduce you to someone who will be helping us out in Thelma's absence. Mr. Samuel Fielding, whom many of you may already know, previously spent ten years as the principal of the high school down the road in Calvin. Sam, come on up here." Sweetwater peered over his glasses at the front of the auditorium, to either side, then the back.

The faculty clapped and Lila noted Anthony Paschetti standing in a side aisle. While everyone else wore polite smiles, his smile fit some other category. Devious? Smug?

And there was no Sam.

The assembled teachers in the auditorium – those that didn't have their heads down surreptitiously grading papers in their laps – looked around, following Sweetwater's gaze to the back to see if the new principal might be there. Meanwhile, Jerome Sweetwater spoke briefly into the walkie talkie that is always close at hand for any inner city administrator. A minute or two elapsed and in came Sam, escorted from the nearby main office by Tiana. "Ah, here he is," said Sweetwater.

Those in the front could hear Tiana say, with a pointed glance at Paschetti, "Someone seems to have told Mr. Fielding that we meet at 3:00, not 2:45."

"Well, no harm done, no harm done," Mr. Sweetwater beckoned Sam forward.

With a broad smile, Sam stepped briskly to the front, his back straight, head high, his military bearing holding him in good stead as he advanced to the front.

"Well, yum, yum," Joyce Ronley crossed her legs, leaning forward slightly as she muttered appraisingly under her breath to Lila. "This could get interesting."

"Really Joyce! Hush." Did Sam look different? Taller? More handsome? Or perhaps it was just seeing him in a different context. "And I didn't think you were attracted to the gray-haired types," hissed Lila.

"Who cares about his hair? I'm looking at what's under it."

Sam shook hands with Mr. Sweetwater and then turned to the assembled teachers. He explained that he was strictly temporary and that like the rest of the faculty, he looked forward to Mrs. Galaska's swift return. He went on to say that he felt assured it would be a smooth transition and for all of them to feel free to approach him with any concerns they might have.

Her voice several notches lower than usual, Joyce said, "My, my, I do love an open door policy."

"Good grief, Joyce. Down, girl." Surely Joyce wasn't trolling for husband number three. It was just Sam, after all.

A few questions followed and the majority of the faculty filed out, a few remaining to have a more direct interaction with Sam. Joyce positioned herself at the front of the group. Waiting in her seat, Lila pulled out the quizzes from her third period class and managed to grade fifteen of them before Sam was finally free. She stuffed them back in her briefcase as he came toward her. She walked with him back to the main office and waited for him to confer briefly with Tiana about the next day, answer a last-minute phone call, and then gather paperwork to be finished at home.

He glanced up from the briefcase on his desk, "This may be our one and only day of car pooling. I know you don't rush out of the door like so many others, but a principal's day runs longer than even the most devoted teacher. I think leaving this early will be a rare luxury for me until I get a handle on things."

"So how'd the day go?"

Sam turned out the overhead light in his office and closed the door. "It had its ups and downs. A young man by the name of Baronoff decided he would not be staying in the in-house detention room and spent some quality time with me in my office."

"I'll bet that was the delightful Leonard. He and I went a few rounds last year. So, it sounds like today was a baptism by fire."

"Well, you were correct about Tiana, who was an enormous help, as was Mrs. Concepcion. Too bad she'll be out on maternity leave so soon. She would be an excellent replacement for Mrs. Galaska."

They were now in the hall and as Sam finished speaking; Lila realized that Anthony Paschetti had been standing by the rear door of the auditorium. Lila wondered if he had heard the last portion of Sam's statement. It would be for the best if he hadn't. Even Paschetti couldn't reasonably expect to be promoted to the position of principal after only eight months as an assistant principal, but he had certainly been sending out signals that he'd like to fill in while Thelma was out. And who ever said the guy was reasonable, anyway?

There appeared to be no limit to his ambition, doubly annoying since it was founded on so little experience and no apparent administrative ability. She'd heard that at his last school he'd somehow catapulted from lowly math teacher to department chairperson in no time, taking the post from someone more qualified, more knowledgeable, and definitely more liked. Word was that he was voted in by using the tactics of charming the new teachers and suggesting the former chair was losing her grip. The possibility of the role he may have played in Thelma's heart attack still hung in her mind.

Conscious of Paschetti's lingering presence, Lila changed the subject to details about her day, and then launched into observations about doings in the town of Calvin. They reached the end of the hall and the doors to the parking lot. She headed outside to her right as Sam paused uncertainly in the doorway. She turned to look back at him.

"What's up, Sam? Do you need to go back for something?"

"No – I don't, I don't see my car. . . ."

"Well, of course not, silly. We drove in together, remember? My heap is over here at the end of the row." She pointed down the line of spaces, now mostly empty. She asked herself if Sam's memory lapse was just absent mindedness at the end of a long day or something more serious.

Sam rubbed the center of his forehead, as if to smooth out the lines between his eyebrows. "Right. Of course. I guess my head was still filled up with school business. How about I thank you for transporting me today with dinner tonight?" Sam opened her door and then went around to the passenger side of the car.

"Sam, I hate to have you cook after your busy day. Come over to my house about 6:30 and I'll come up with something – I do make a pretty good pasta primavera. That ought to meet with your approval."

"That sounds fine and I believe I have a loaf of zucchini bread I can contribute. I need to use up all that zucchini somehow; I had a bumper crop this year."

Lila pulled into the city traffic, mentally rounding up the asparagus and other necessary vegetables for dinner.

# CHAPTER EIGHT

Lila stacked the dishes by the sink to deal with later, thinking to herself that Sam had appeared tired that evening, but why not? Even the most strenuous hours in a garden were very different from time spent behind a desk, putting out bureaucratic fires, and dealing with wayward youth, distraught parents, and jumpy faculty.

She wrapped up the leftover zucchini bread that Sam had insisted she keep. At least he had eaten well, even taking some of her oatmeal cookies back with him for later. Good thing, since even though he had always been lean and hard-muscled, lately he had been looking way too thin. She suspected his vegan diet was to blame. Perhaps she could enlist the services of Nahiomi, head of the cafeteria ladies at school, to ply him with fattening treats.

And speaking of fattening, her jeans had been feeling a little snug – a walk after dinner might not be a bad idea. It was still early enough. Sam had gone home shortly after eating, it being a school night for both of them now, and the light had not yet faded.

She gathered up her iPod, tied a sweatshirt around her waist for the incoming evening chill, and opened the screen door. Winston slipped out ahead of her to stare at some promising holes by the stone wall. Six wild turkeys, all hens, flapped noisily up from the acorns beneath the oak to the trees surrounding the yard, their large dark shapes looking incongruous and even a little ominous on the branches against the sky.

She headed down Old County Road toward Main, listening to the latest mystery she'd downloaded from the library, which was about the only way she had time for leisure "reading" when school was in session. Since her end of town was mostly woods, with only a few older farmhouses, she had the road to herself. It was freeing to be outside instead of hunkered over a pile of papers in her living room. But she'd need to get in to school a little early to finish up those quizzes if she wanted to hand them back the next day. She had learned that a promptly graded paper had way more impact than one handed back to students weeks later. And another thing - she'd have more control over her arrival time since she didn't have to pick up Sam.

Thinking about Sam brought her thoughts to her friend Joyce, who had certainly been revving up her amatory engines that day. Lila's pace quickened. And why not? she asked herself, striding even more quickly. Sam was a perfectly presentable example of the male species, in fact one of its better representatives. Who could argue against six foot three of lean muscle, thick pepper and salt hair, and a warm, honest smile? She pictured Joyce hanging on Sam's arm, batting her eyelashes at him while he looked down at her. She found that she had lost her place in the recording and was now jogging, not her intent when she had decided on a leisurely evening stroll. She slowed to a walk, telling herself that what Sam did was his own business. Lila crossed Main Street, heading left towards Calvin High. She passed the school's weather-beaten sign and turned into the drive while trying to reverse her audio player to a point she recognized. She glanced up and saw a blue contractor's truck in the curved drive. A man in jeans and work boots, his sweatshirt rolled up at the sleeves, was loading large buckets in the back and he turned his head in her direction as she approached.

A brief moment passed as they both put on the polite half smiles used to greet a stranger. Pausing, bucket in hand, the man cocked his head slightly to the side. She stopped walking.

"Lila?"

"Toby?"

"Amazing. Last time I saw you was right here, the end of your senior year. You were spouting off about getting the hell out of Calvin, shaking our farm dust from your heels."

The years had been kind to Toby Giavanelli. He still had a full head of that blue-black hair and his shoulders were as powerful as ever. Aside from a bit more real estate around his middle, he hadn't changed markedly from the defense tackle he'd been in high school, big even then as a sophomore to her senior.

"Yeah, well here I am, back again. After college I stayed in the D.C. area until my parents passed away a few years ago. I thought I was just organizing the house for sale but somehow I never left. Guess I finally grew up enough to look around and appreciate what's here."

"Oh gee, that's right, Lila. I'd forgotten. I was sorry to hear about your parents."

"So - what are you up to? And what are you doing here at the school?"

"I've been putting another layer of tar on this worn-out roof. One of my workmen did a crappy patch job and Mrs. Rothberger's room – remember how we always thought she wore a wig? – developed its own personal Niagara Falls. I hope it holds now. Really, that roof should be replaced. This building's going to start disintegrating, one leak at a time, unless some money starts rolling into the area and the town sees fit to spend it on the school. It worries me. With Toni about to have Giavanelli number four, I need to know there's going to be somewhere our kids can get educated."

"Congratulations, Toby. Four? That's incredible. I'm still looking around for that perfect guy."

"As I recall, you were looking in high school, too. Plenty of guys interested, but you were pretty choosy."

She thought back to those days; she had always had a date for a party or prom, but had never settled on any one boy. Looked like she hadn't changed much over the years.

"Well, I remember you and Toni were certainly inseparable in high school and now here you are still together. Hey, say hi to Toni for me; maybe I could stop by for a visit after the baby's born."

Toby lifted the last bucket into the bag of the van, pushed the door closed and smiled down at Lila. "Great idea. Toni's always happy to have a real adult to talk to and with four boys, a female adult would be even better."

He climbed into the driver's seat, Lila reinserted her ear buds, and they each departed, Toby for Main Street, Lila for the school track.

Surely two laps were enough to cancel out those last five oatmeal cookies, Lila reasoned. Guilt assuaged, she returned down Old County, still listening to her audio book. After failing to inform anyone else where she would be, the heroine in her mystery was of course now alone in a darkened church yard. In the deepening twilight Lila stared ahead, wondering if the story's handsome local constable had divined the owner of the fatal hat pin, or if perhaps the lonely, and also handsome, aristocrat might choose this evening to languish at his wife's grave. Joining the heroine was the harmless old spinster who had suddenly developed a manic gleam in her eye:

*"'And so you see my dear, I'm so very sorry. You seemed like such a sweet thing; such a pity. . .'"*

Feeling a blow to her left shoulder, she found herself falling sideways and fruitlessly grabbing for anything to slow her descent. Her right knee crunched down into the gravel at the edge of the road. While still trying to process what had happened, she felt big hands on her shoulders, pulling her to her feet.

"OW! What the hell?! Who ? –"

"I called out; you must not have heard me. Let me brush you off."

"What? Wait! Stop that!" Lila yanked the earphones from her head, slapping at the hands on her back as she looked up.

Grey hooded eyes topped by curls topaz in the dim light smiled down at her.

"You! Perfect." It was that Thanasomething guy from the post office. She stepped away and leaned down to look at her leg. The knee of her jeans was dirty, with a small rip. "Even better - my favorite jeans. Any particular reason why you knocked me off my feet into what will undoubtedly turn out to be poison ivy?"

"I was running and in the dusk must have miscalculated how close I was. I am your new neighbor, Nikolaos Athanasopoulos, but of course you must call me Niko. I am so, so sorry. I must correct this. Please come to my house; see, my driveway is just here." There was a faint trace of accent in his speech. He seemed determined to keep his hand at her elbow, and after snatching her arm away once, she surrendered. She had discovered that she was a tad unsteady and the solidity of the arm next to her resembled a limb on the oak in her yard. Limping slightly, but still unwilling to let go of her anger, she first allowed herself to be led across the road, but then changed her mind.

"Look, I'm fine and my driveway is just there opposite yours." At this declaration of fitness her knee collapsed under her and only his quick reflexes saved her from another union with the road surface. Suddenly she was airborne and traveling four feet above the ground as he picked her up, apparently effortlessly. "This is not necessary! Put me down!"

"Let us just wait until we have a look at that knee." Implacably, he continued to carry her down his driveway.

*** 

A very short time later, her leg elevated on a sleek blonde footstool, crystal tumbler of water in hand, Lila sat back and scanned her surroundings. The huge sunroom filled with expensive furniture had certainly not been here when the Weatherills owned the house. They had been what might be called 'casual decorators' - both inside and out. They had never quite reached the refrigerator-on-the-porch stage, but any object used in a twenty-four hour period was likely to still be where it was last seen, and an extroverted assortment of dogs had usually wandered sociably among the broken lawn furniture and bicycle parts in the big front yard.

She had seen other signs of her new neighbor's efforts as he had helped her to the sunroom. Hardwood floors gleamed, walls were freshly painted, and it looked as though new windows had been installed throughout. He had certainly transformed this house. That must have been the sounds of construction Sam had heard. Judging by what she'd seen so far, cost apparently wasn't a concern. She wondered what other changes Niko had in mind and if they were limited to the house itself.

He had provided her with an ice pack for her knee and insisted that she rest for a few moments before returning home. The subtle recessed lighting glinted off his hair, but failed to illuminate his hooded eyes. Just sitting there quietly in grey and black workout gear, he exuded confidence. What was someone like him doing here?

Lila said, "So what is someone like you doing here? Calvin isn't exactly a hub of activity. The town is mostly populated by young families or people who grew up here and didn't have the gumption to leave."

"Ah, but it is a lovely town. Still so much unspoiled land, so many beautiful places to see."

"Is that what drew you here? The land?"

Niko leaned forward, smiling. "Ah yes. The land, the neighbors." He tipped his head and raised those blond eyebrows. "And it appears I have a neighbor before me?"

"Oh, yes. Sorry. I'm Lila. Lila Wallace."

His smile deepened, "Hello, Lila Wallace. I have already met my other neighbor, Mr. Samuel Fielding; our lands touch. He seems to have an exceptionally large garden. Does he farm all of his land?"

"No. Sam's a high school principal – or was – or is." Lila brushed a long tendril of hair behind her ear. "It's complicated. He ran Calvin High for years but quit when his wife was dying. Now he's filling in at my high school in the city. And that garden was the only way Sam kept going after May died. I think he likes having the land because he and his wife used to spend so much time just walking around the fields together."

"Such a sad story. Perhaps it would be better not to possess the fields that take him to sad memories." His face wore a look of concern and he shook his head slowly.

She thought he seemed uncommonly interested in Sam and his land. And what difference did it make to him what Sam did with his fields? She noticed he hadn't asked about her property or, for that matter, much about the rest of the area. Was it Sam's land that he was after? And why? The guy was obviously no farmer. She realized that she had learned little about him. She seemed to be dispensing more information than she was acquiring.

"Well, you've been very kind, but I must be going. Tomorrow is a work day for me. I imagine you'll also need to be getting up early?" She waited for him to provide a similar sketch of his day.

"This visit was much too short and I still do not feel I have rectified my terrible actions. Would you be able to have dinner with me? I will cook for you - good Greek food that will make you strong for exercise." Still no information, she thought.

"Fine. Perhaps one night this week? Thursday?" Might as well get it over with, she told herself. Maybe she could ply him with his own wine and get to the bottom of what this inscrutable and obviously high-powered man was doing in the sleepy bedroom community of Calvin.

"Wonderful! Now I shall drive you home. No, do not argue. Do you think you are able to walk to the door here? It leads to the parking area for my cars."

She stood up gingerly, testing her knee for stability. Sore but serviceable.

She managed to enter and exit the enormous SUV under her own steam, a point for her side, or at least for her dignity. Her self-regard faltered a little when she realized how much she liked the subtle warmth of the heater in the leather seat, not to mention silently gliding high above the pot-holed country road. He had still insisted on helping her up her front steps, and then had taken both her hands in his and looked across at her with his unreadable grey eyes.

"I know that we shall become the best of friends, Lila Wallace." Still holding her hands, he gave her a long searching look. "Until Thursday!"

She pulled her hands from his grasp and dragged her eyes from his, turning to her door. "Um, yeah, right. See you Thursday."

She had hobbled into her house at this point, but when she looked back he was still standing there, watching her intently even as she closed the door on him.

Sheesh, she thought. Such drama.

# CHAPTER NINE

"Mudak! Idiots!" This was punctuated by a loud bang on one of the metal school lockers outside Lila's classroom door. "Dermo!"

Lila was sitting at her desk, resting her still-sore knee, and she wasn't certain what some of those words meant, but she was pretty sure it wasn't anything good. Next she heard Maura-Mary O'Shaughnessy trying to soothe whoever it was out in the hall. She wasn't able to make out much of what was being said. It was a mix of English and Russian. Fortunately, it was her prep period so she stepped out of her room to see if M&M needed some support, or perhaps even defense. There were mailboxes taller than Ms. O'Shaughnessy.

Standing quietly nearby, she might as well have been invisible to the enraged student and the teacher who was trying to calm him. M&M kept her hands to herself, but leaned in slightly, "Leonard, I know you're upset. I know it's wrong for Terrance and Roberto to comment on the way you speak. Their behavior just shows ignorance. But we need to find a way to help you deal with this that doesn't get you thrown out of class."

After one or two more thumps on the locker interspersed with quiet counseling by Ms. O'Shaughnessy, the issue was somewhat resolved, or at least less explosive, and they stepped back into Mr. Lemur's nearby history class. Lila returned to her own room and settled at her desk, trying to regroup her thoughts.

Her lesson plan book awaited her. Which to start with this year? Dickinson, Frost, or Whitman? They were all pretty accessible, but Dickinson's poems were short, and as a result often tricked the poetry-phobic into thinking that a poetry unit might be survivable. Wait until they realized the layers upon layers of meaning to be found in the simplest line of Miss Emily, she thought.

The bell came too soon, and she went out to the hall where she joined Bill Moynihan, who was kidding with a student over the merits and deficiencies of their chosen NBA teams. The boy went off smiling to his next class, stopping on the way to do the obligatory and intricate handshake when he met a friend. Bill resumed his paternal surveillance of the busy corridor.

She noted Warren Brown down the hall at Stella Slocumb's locker; not a pairing she would have expected. Both were nice kids, but Warren's school work showed genuine thought, whereas the best that could be said about Stella's was that it was invariably neat and on time. It was a little surprising to still see Warren in the hall; he was usually the first into her class. However, this looked to be an extended conversation. The girl's head was down, her hand tracing patterns on the metal locker while the boy bent his head to hear her.

"So we had a little excitement out in the hall last period. Leonard again, huh?"

"Yeah. I stepped out to check on it but M&M had everything under control. I feel sorry for Leonard. I'm not sure why he's been chosen as Terrance's and Roberto's victim. Roberto doesn't speak English all that well himself, and even though Terrance was born right here in the city, his own command of the language is pretty weak."

"Bullies like to see a reaction Lila, and with that temper, Leonard has proven to be fertile ground."

"Well, they'd better be careful. Leonard's no pushover – he runs with a tough crowd, all Russian. This could easily result in more than a few dented lockers."

"Not to worry. I'm sure Paschetti has it well in hand."

"Good thing I know you're kidding, Bill, or I might doubt your sanity. Can you imagine him counseling anyone? After a session with him, a kid would start looking for a back-street arms dealer. Remember that pep rally when he tried to intervene in the name-calling between the Hispanic and black gang kids? We nearly had a riot until Mr. Sweetwater stepped in."

"Yeah, that was a close one. And yet he's well-versed in "intervention strategies", or at least that's what he'll tell you if you stand still long enough."

Lila's class had almost finished filing into the room, Stella and Warren slipping in just before the bell. As she entered and closed the door, she called back to Mr. Moynihan, "If that's who we're depending on, we're all doomed."

It was the last period of the day. She was doing her utmost to sustain the class's interest in the lesson, but with the warm afternoon sun steaming in, she'd need to leap onto her desk and perhaps knock out a Flamenco routine or two to get their attention. Some students wrote with their heads resting on an arm flung across the desk. Sasha Fowlkes, one of her best students, stifled a yawn, while William Pena, abandoning all pretenses, had his head down completely. It sometimes seemed as though the window of opportunity to grab their consciousness covered only about two and a half hours in the school day, if that. Still, she had to hand out the poetry assignments before the bell rang.

"Stella, you have 'A narrow fellow in the grass' and 'I took my power in my hand.'"

"Jacob, you. . . . "

Her next instructions were drowned out by the overhead speaker, this time Tiana in the main office. "Will Mr. Fielding please report to the office, Mr. Fielding please report to the office."

She resumed her assignments: "Jacob, your poems are 'Hope is the thing with feathers' and 'After great pain, a formal feeling comes.'"

Her desk phone rang, and she looked at the clock, exasperated. She still needed to make the assignment clear before they left. She sighed and picked up the receiver.

"Ms. Wallace, 306."

"Ms. Wallace? Have you seen Mr. Fielding? I have Dr. Daniele here from Central Office to meet with him and he is not answering his page."

"Did you try his walkie-talkie?"

"Yes. I don't understand. He has it with him."

"Gee, I'm sorry, Tiana. I have no idea where he might be."

The class was busy packing up their belongings, waiting like runners for the gun. Maybe thirty seconds were left of the day. "Okay, so you each have two poems by Dickinson. Next class — yes, next class! — you must explicate one of them thoroughly for the class's benefit. That information will then be included in the test we'll be having, so you'll also want to bring your note-taking skills."

Youthful groaning mingled with the bell and the scraping of chairs and they were gone.

Lila gathered up the leftover handouts, and walked through the room straightening desks and rescuing a forgotten sweater from beneath a chair. She wondered what had happened with Sam. Had some of his mental fogginess come with him to school? No, she told herself, he was probably just tangled up in some other part of the building, but then it wasn't like him to blow off an important meeting.

On a hunch, she locked her classroom door and headed for the gym, the one place in the huge school where you couldn't hear announcements from the main office. When she pulled open the door she saw Sam and two very tall young men in conversation, each at least two inches taller than their principal. One boy leaned forward aggressively at the waist, the other clenched and unclenched his fists, staring at the polished wooden gym floor.

". . . and that is the end of this, Jamal, or you will both be receiving three-day suspensions which will be scheduled to coincide with whatever game we have coming up. Is that clear enough for you, Jesus?" Both students sullenly nodded their heads, studiously looking away from each other. "Okay, in-house suspension tomorrow for both of you. You will also work together to create two new plays for the team. You will do this under the supervision of Coach Cleary to ensure that you both contribute equally.

Off you go."

After a pause, they lumbered out with much swaggering but each keeping a healthy distance from the other.

Watching them leave, Sam glanced over as Lila approached and allowed himself a twitch of a smile. "Not bad boys, just both ambitious to be the starting forward. A minor disagreement that they hoped to blow up into something larger."

"Sam, Tiana's been trying to reach you. Margaret Daniele has a meeting with you – she's been here for over twenty minutes."

"I haven't heard any pages and my walkie-talkie's been quiet."

"There's no speaker in the gym, so that explains why you didn't hear the pages. Call the office and let Tiana know that you're on your way."

Sam pulled the device from where it was hooked on his belt. "Home base. This is Fielding." Nothing; no static or squawk. Sam tried again. Still nothing. Using a key from his pocket, he pried open the back. There were no batteries at all. It was empty.

"Well, look at this. No wonder I haven't been getting any messages."

"That's just weird, but right now you've got to get to the library. I can't imagine what Dr. Daniele is thinking. You don't want downtown to think you're unreliable. I'll call the library from the Phys Ed office."

They both went in opposite directions, Lila walking quickly across the polished floor while Sam broke into a trot.

Arriving at the library, Sam headed for the conference room where he found Assistant Principal Paschetti leaning back expansively in one of the chairs as Margaret Daniele watched him, expressionless. "I'm sure you'll agree with me, Dr. Daniele, that Thomas Paine High School needs dependable leadership. I'm glad I was in the office when our secretary was trying to reach Mr. Fielding. I'll be happy to help with any information you may require."

Sam stood in the doorway, taking in the scene. "Hello, Dr. Daniele and thank you, Mr. Paschetti. I can take it from here. Unfortunately I was delayed by a student confrontation between two of our juniors. Isn't the junior class your area of responsibility, Anthony? I think you should go over to the gym and make sure they left the school grounds without incident."

Paschetti's chair came down with a thump as he looked up at the doorway in surprise. "Oh! Yes! Of course." Sam wondered if there could be a connection between Paschetti's surprise at seeing him and the missing batteries.

Sam took a chair at the table as the assistant principal scuttled out.

Having returned to her room, Lila settled at her desk to answer emails and sort papers for the next day. An hour later, the room began to dim in the autumn light and she gathered her coat, purse, lunch bag and briefcase and left, locking her classroom door. She started to take the staircase closest to the parking lot but then decided she'd check to see how Sam's meeting had gone. She headed toward the front of the building, passing mostly darkened rooms. The art room still had kids there, some working on projects, others were friends who just needed a place to hang out after school. There weren't always many safe options in the city.

She reached the main office and waved to Tiana who was just putting on her coat. "He still here?"

"Yes, Miss. He's in his office." The secretary smiled from the door. "Good night."

"Night, Tiana."

She popped her head in Sam's office and found him standing by his desk, a post-it note in his hand. She walked in and glanced at the paper. "'Problem in gym. Please stop by this afternoon.' That's odd. Why would Paschetti ask you to go to the gym?"

"Why do you say Mr. Paschetti wrote this?"

"Oh, we all know his handwriting – he likes to drop 'helpful hints' in our mailboxes. Why did he want you to go to the gym?"

"I have no idea, but I have a suspicion."

"Well, I wanted you to draw your own conclusions about the staff, Sam, but he's someone you might want to keep your eye on."

Sam's forehead wrinkled briefly and then he smiled down at her. "Yes, I think I agree. Let's go home, shall we? It's been a long day."

He just looked so decent and dependable standing there, his shoulders back, his jaw firm, and still with that twinkle lurking in those blue eyes. She smiled back and nodded. "Home it is."

# CHAPTER TEN

The next morning, in spite of a large dose of tea, a still-groggy Lila reached into the fridge and pulled out the ingredients for that day's lunch: a container of yogurt plus a pear for later in the day. She grabbed two baggies and filled one with pretzels, and in the other, the incentive to get through this boring lunch, two hefty brownies, dropping all in her blue lunch sack.

Her heavier jacket on – before long she'd need the giant puffy coat – she went out of the kitchen door, and then the screened porch door. She narrowly missed stepping on a large garter snake lying on the big granite block that served as the step into the house. After some fast footwork she regained her balance. Winston! The cat was nowhere to be seen, but she'd recognize his handiwork anywhere. How else would a snake get there when the temperatures had been dropping into the low forties at night? Every other snake with any sense was tucked deep in a stone wall, or under her porch. This thought sent her rapidly off to her car and she opened its back door. Blinking up at her was Winston. She had left the back window open, and the car must have held enough residual heat from yesterday's warm temperatures to be tempting. She shooed him out and piled her various objects in.

She backed down the driveway but as she pulled into Old County Road she spotted Niko, who must have walked down his drive to collect his newspaper. Bother, thought Lila. Nothing to be done except to say hello.

She rolled down the passenger window and called across the console. "Good morning, Niko. You're up and about early. Are you off to an important meeting?" He had on a rich grey suit, which she bet would match his eyes on closer inspection. My goodness, but he did look - um - handsome standing there. She found she wasn't really listening to his reply as he walked toward her car.

" - miss paper delivery to the house. Country living is very different. But walking to gather the paper can be a fine way to begin the day, don't you agree? Especially when I find a lovely sight such as you at the end of my walk."

Again no straight answer to her question. "Yes. I mean, nice to see you, too."

He was now leaning in her passenger window, his hand resting on the car. Yep, she thought, the suit was the same grey as his eyes, and they were focused keenly on her. "Do not forget our appointment tonight. I will cook good Greek food for you!" Niko smiled, and even in the early-morning dimness his teeth shone like alabaster.

Whoa - this all felt a bit intense for so early in the morning but Lila returned his smile, "Uh, sure. Yep! See you then! Well, gotta go!"

Niko stepped back, still smiling as she rolled the window up and drove away. Involuntarily, she looked up at her rear-view mirror and saw him standing there in the morning light. She exhaled, noticing her heart rate had increased.

Turning on to Main, Lila decided she needed another cup of tea for the road and, with the experienced wisdom of a townie, she slowed down as she drew near Binding-Stevens Market. Thanks to the angled parking, the area in front of the store was rich with potential accidents. Less wary drivers were often seen slamming on their brakes as apparently stationary vehicles suddenly reversed blindly from their parking spots into oncoming traffic. Added to this, pedestrians would dash out in the blithe belief that an orange crosswalk painted on the road would actually provide safety. Why the strengthening morning light wasn't reflected in pools of blood was a mystery to her.

Toby Giavanelli was tentatively backing out his company truck. She stopped and signaled for him to continue. Recognizing her, he waved a thank you out of his window and drove off, ladders clanking. She pulled into the now vacant spot and when she walked up the steps toward the double screen door she could already hear the buzz of conversation inside. The store only closed its heavier outer doors in the coldest weather; the heat of cooking and number of bodies inside usually made an open door necessary.

Libby Brannan, a tall strawberry blonde in her late twenties and a hard-working grad student, was behind the counter as usual and was deep in discussion with the beloved town patriarch, ninety-five-year-old Josiah Woods.

"I mean, back in my day, Mr. Woods, that building was in sad shape. You could break your neck tripping on the peeling floor tiles in the school library and half the outside doors had to be chained just to make sure they closed. So I can't even imagine what it must be like now – Hi Lila, how are you?" She broke away from her conversation with Josiah to greet Lila, then turned as quickly to call across the store. "George. George! Your order's ready!"

A tall man in jeans and quilted jacket wearing an impressively heavy tool belt pushed away from a table populated by two other men, one in a three piece suit, the other in running gear. The early-morning crew ran the gamut through all professions, lawyers to plumbers, with a smattering of retirees. George peered into the bag handed across the counter to him and in the voice of one to whom this had happened before, said, "This isn't what I ordered, Libby."

Libby took back the offending bag, handed it to a woman tapping her foot and talking on a cell phone, then deftly flipped a fried egg onto the English muffin that had emerged from the toaster at that instant, added a grilled tomato and slice of cheese, wrapped it all in aluminum foil, placed it in another bag and handed it to George. She returned to the debate with Josiah as money traveled from hands to the register. ". . so what we need is to get this on the town warrant that's coming up for vote soon. Or that high school is just going to fall down in a pile of bricks and chalk dust one day."

Still leaning on the counter, Josiah grinned and shifted his weight. "Your day? When did you graduate from Calvin High, Libby? Seven, eight years ago? In my day it wasn't even there. Why, we had to go all the way into the city if we wanted to go to high school. Either that or find the money to attend the Academy here in town. Not many of us farming kids could do that."

Libby turned to Lila, "So Lila, what'll it be?"

"A tall Earl Grey and one of those bear claws, please Libby. Hi, Josiah, good to see you."

"Got it," Fluidly, Libby leaned into the pastry showcase and dropped the sticky sweet roll into a white waxed bag. "Well, all I know is we need some new money in this town, Mr. Woods. Lots of families and houses but not much in the way of business to bring in revenue." She pulled the clear coffee pot of simmering water from the burner, dropped a tea bag into a cup and filled it, slapping on a plastic lid.

Josiah sipped his coffee. "Watch out what you wish for. Word's goin' round that there might just be some kind of commercial venture starting up. I'd hate to see our woods and fields disappear for some shopping center. My land's about the last real farm here in Calvin."

Lila, mindful of the time, managed to pay with exact change and turned to leave in spite of her interest in the conversation. She'd rather have stayed to hear about this commercial venture Josiah was talking about. Now that she'd come back to town she had a heartfelt interest in preserving Calvin's open spaces. As she picked up her bag and cup of tea the screen door opened to admit a blond Texas-haired woman of indeterminate age. Real estate agent Arlene Gerrigan, her trademark scarf tangled as usual in the reading glasses hanging about her neck, called out, "Well, hello to you all! What a lovely morning, don't you agree? Lila, how is that big old farmhouse? Thinking you might want to move to something more practical?"

"No, Arlene. Thanks for asking, but no sale. I'm happy where I am. Now I'd better get going."

Trying to exit, she found herself caught in a minuet with Arlene, whose briefcase strap had somehow caught on Lila's sleeve. As they rotated about, trying to disengage, Josiah called over, "Arlene! As a realtor, you ought to know. What do you hear about some kind of land speculatin' around here?"

Arlene's partially zippered briefcase had now begun disgorging company pens and copies of house listings onto the wide plank floor. "Oh my! Ha, Ha! Well, I'm sure I have no idea. (Here, Lila, if you could just lift this strap a little bit more onto my shoulder – there, that ought to do it) When there is something to report, you just know that I'll let you know." A sudden burst of the 1983's hit 'Our House' filled the store. "Oh dear, was that my phone or yours that I just heard?"

Finally able to step out of Arlene's sphere of falling objects and protruding straps, Lila headed to her car, the realtor's protestations of ignorance still audible through the door. It seemed Sam had also decided on a traveling breakfast, for he had just pulled into the spot next to hers. She waited for him to emerge from his car. "Morning, Lila. Picking up something for the road, too?"

"Hi, Sam. Yeah, I figured I'd stoke up on sugar and caffeine to give me a jump start to face my classes. Speaking of which, I'd better get going. I got slowed down by the morning gossip. Josiah's in there trying to pry some information out of Arlene. It seems somebody's looking to start some kind of commercial thing here in Calvin."

"Huh. I hadn't heard that. I wonder where? Funny thing is, that new neighbor of ours seemed mighty curious the other day about my back acres."

She turned from opening her car door and paused. "What did he say?"

"Oh, nothing definite. Just asking how many acres I had and if they reached that rail line like his land does. I know you've got to get going, but why don't you stop by after school and we'll have pot luck tonight and talk

94

about it?"

She avoided his eye by fussing with placement of the container of tea in the cup holder of her car. She next put the pastry bag on the passenger seat. "Um, I can't tonight, Sam. I'm actually going over to Niko's." Shoot, she thought. Why couldn't she just lie? She used to be pretty good at keeping her arrangements with one guy secret from another. Sam's inherent honesty must be infectious.

The corners of his mouth lifted, but it wasn't quite enough to trigger the usual smile lines at his eyes. "That's fine. Maybe another time. Better get my coffee and get going, too. See you at school." Sam turned into the building. She gave herself a little shake and settled herself in the car for the ride into the city.

*** 

On her way home from school that afternoon Lila made a spur of the moment decision and pulled into the driveway of the Calvin town offices. They were in a smallish white frame building, not particularly official, but blending in well with the nearby historic houses. Pulling open the door, she entered into a narrow hallway with a maze of doors opening off of it, each one with a sign attached to the wall indicating what was housed in each office. A woman who must have been signing up the two kids with her for fall sports emerged from Park and Rec. Both boys, one about seven, the other perhaps nine, followed behind her and were giggling and playing at trying to trip the other as they walked. Shallow showcases on one wall listed senior center activities, displayed the town charter, and held trophies for town achievements of the past.

On the other side of the hallway were framed photographs of Calvin's earlier days. She passed a doorway with its sign announcing that this was the location to get dump stickers and turned into the next one labeled Town Assessors Office.

Seeing Arlene that morning and hearing the rumors of land development in town and then hearing that Niko had been questioning Sam about his land had made her curious. She stepped up to the counter and a small woman with improbably red hair and a World's Best Grandma bedazzled sweatshirt came from behind a cluttered desk in response. Lila was suddenly transported to fifth grade, Girl Scout badges, and Mrs. Bugnacki leading the troop in singing, "Make New Friends."

"Why, is this Lila Wallace? It's so good to see you, dear. I was so sorry to hear about your parents. Such a shame. They were so devoted to each other. And now you're in that big house? Well, my, my. What can I do for you, honey?"

"Hello Mrs. Bugnacki. I was wondering if I could see some plot plans from my area?"

"Of course you can. Getting to know the old neighborhood, are you? And why not? It's all yours now. Good to know what you've got. I'll them right now." She turned to a tall cabinet on her left, opening the doors to reveal stacks of narrow shelves that were filled with big sheets of paper. "That's Old County Road, right? What's your number?" She looked over her shoulder, cocking her head like an alert bird, her earrings of tiny teapots swinging.

"Um, no. I'm looking for 78 and 98 Old County."

"Oh! Well, fine. As a resident in town you have the right to look at anything you want. Now let me see. . ." She lifted the glasses that were on a chain around her neck, perching them on the end of her nose. "Okay, here we go. . . Old County. 78 and 98?" She sifted through the stack and then emerged with two large sheets, bringing them to the counter. "Here you go, honey."

Mrs. Bugnacki paused, as though hoping for an extended conversation. Lila smiled, "Thanks so much." Dismissed, the woman returned to her desk. Lila spread them out before her, side by side. It was interesting; the plans matched like two pieces of a puzzle. Not much to see, really. The rail line did in fact cut through the back of both Niko and Sam's property, something she already knew from wandering the fields as a kid. She wasn't sure what she had been expecting to find. Some detective she was. She stacked the sheets and called across to the clerk.

"I guess I'm done. Sorry to have troubled you."

The woman bustled up the counter, smiling. "No trouble at all. It was a treat to see you." She gathered up the papers and carried them to the cabinet.

Lila paused in the doorway. "Mrs. Bugnacki? Has anyone else been asking about these lately?"

"Well, funny you should ask. Someone was just here the other day. Big fella, blond hair."

#

Stretched out on her couch, Lila leaned back and closed her eyes. It had been a pretty good day at school; a surprising number of her students had actually done the reading assigned for homework and outside of a small flare-up in the lunchroom between Leonard and Terrance, peace had reigned. But still Lila was tired and she wished she could bow out of dinner with Niko, particularly now that her suspicions about him had deepened. She reminded herself that the purpose of the evening was investigative. It was almost six and time to get ready. Unwillingly, she lifted a limp and sleepy Winston from her lap and stood up.

She went upstairs and told herself she would not over-think her clothes. It was only Thursday night after all, and not a real date. She would just have a quick dinner and then get back to her couch. What to wear? An outfit somewhere between weeding the garden and deliberate seduction was needed. She pulled her black velveteen jeans from the closet, rejected her deep blue silk shirt, and drew her grey V-necked sweater over her head. After a glance in the mirror, she tied a gold and silver scarf around her neck to discourage any possible hint of cleavage. Gold hoop earrings, gold bracelet, black flats, and that would just have to do it.

Back downstairs she looked through the sidelights of the front door to see Niko just arriving at her doorstep, the light from the porch light caught in his curls. She paused for a breath, tossed on her camel hair car coat, drew on her gloves, and opened her door to his wide smile and admiring gaze. What a smile, she thought. This perplexing man with his mysterious plans was way too tantalizing. Exactly the type she really should avoid and yet too often was drawn to. It would be so much simpler (and safer!) to just stay home. With an envious glance at Winston, who had contentedly circled back into a warm plush pile on the couch, she pulled the door closed behind her.

\*\*\*

Dinner had not been at all what she had expected. Yes, there had been the requisite candles, and yes, soft music, but it took place in the kitchen, not the formal dining room she could see through the doorway. Niko completed the finishing touches while Lila sat on a tall wrought iron stool at the granite island and sipped a deep red wine, watching him mix a sauce of cucumbers and yogurt. He then handed her the sauce and a basket of warm pita bread, lifted a colorful pottery casserole from the oven, and led her to a round table pushed up to an inviting window seat in an alcove of the kitchen. The bottle of the wine was already on the table, along with a salad in an earthenware bowl. It turned out to be an unpretentious meal of keftedes, which he explained were simply meatballs, made of lamb with hints of garlic and mint.

She'd had a day filled with the cacophony of teen age voices and harsh bells ringing every hour, and she thought she might just send out roots and anchor herself permanently right here in these soft pillows. She dug in slightly with her shoulders and felt her eyes close as the music drifted in from the other room.

Whoops. She opened her eyes to see Niko moving in across the pillows. She began to retreat, but to where? Her back was already against the big bay window. Then she realized that he was simply refilling her wine glass.

"A difficult day at school?" His direct gaze and tilted head demonstrated sympathy.

She hadn't noticed before how low his voice was, musical even.

She pulled herself into a more upright position and, to break the spell she felt descending, reached for another section of pita. "No, not really. I think it's just the end of the day at the end of the week. It's a cumulative effect." His warm hand brushed hers as he placed his napkin on the table. She needed to remember that her mission tonight was to gather information. "How was your day? You looked to be going somewhere important when I saw you this morning."

He smiled at her and his eyelids dropped slightly, giving him the sleepy expression of a big cat temporarily at rest. "Ah, business. So very boring and there are so many more interesting topics." He lifted a deep blue pillow that separated the two of them and positioned it at her back.

"Well, you know, it's so funny! That was exactly the topic of conversation in town center this morning." A defense tactic of wide-eyed perkiness kicked in to hopefully counteract his seductive campaign of charm. "People are wondering about the rumors of new business coming to Calvin. Do you know anything about that?"

A hint of annoyance crossed his face. He rose to move their plates to the kitchen counter. He busied himself with a complicated-looking coffee maker before he answered. "If we must talk of such things, I will say that, yes, I am looking for a location suitable for many companies. I believe you would call it a business park. Perhaps now some coffee and Metaxa?" Raising a blond eyebrow, he held up a tall, slim bottle with a golden label.

He brought mugs and what looked to be shot glasses to the table. If alcohol would loosen his tongue, thought Lila, she was willing to take the risk. She said, "So where is this going to be? Our town certainly needs the revenue that a business park would bring, but I'd hate to see us lose our hiking trails or farm land." Would he admit to his interest in Sam's land, she wondered?

"Do not concern yourself, dear lady. Nothing is decided, it is still just thoughts and dreams and talk and ideas." His face was close to hers and his words were almost hypnotic. "Cream?" The coffee was aromatic even for a tea-drinker like her, and upon a cautious sip of the brandy, her mouth filled with the tastes of spices and sunshine. He settled again on the window seat. The space between them seemed to have diminished. The brandy traveled warmly through her system; it was heady after a long day at work. She reached for what she hoped would be a bracing dose of coffee, but became aware of his arm across the pillows at her back. Was she imagining the heat radiating from that solid form next to her or was it the brandy? She didn't need to turn to know that he was looking at her. At least she'd pried out a little information. She put down her coffee cup quickly. "My goodness, it's getting quite late and I still have another work day ahead of me. I really should be getting home. Thank you for a lovely meal, Niko." She slid across the banquette and scanned the room for her jacket.

"I am so sorry you must leave so soon. This evening has been so very, very enjoyable." He held her jacket for her to slip on and she could feel his breath on her neck. She put one arm in a sleeve, then the other. His hands remained on her shoulders for an extra beat and then he released her. A small shiver traveled across her back. They walked to the door and Lila protested as he started to put on his own coat.

"No, really, Niko. I'm fine. In fact I think I'd prefer to walk home by myself. I need to clear my head after that wine and brandy!"

"I cannot send you out into the night alone."

She attempted a light-hearted laugh. "Into the mean streets of

Calvin? I'll be fine."

A brief skirmish and they compromised; he would escort her to the end of his drive. She gave in, figuring she could resist his allure and her own impulses at least long enough to make it to the road.

Having finally escaped from the temptations of Niko, Lila stood quietly in the dark. It was hushed under the stars. The noise of a busy summer night filled with chatting insects was now long gone. All that remained was the sound of a breeze in the very tops of the pine trees.

"May! May, is that you there?"

"Sam?" A tall figure was silhouetted in the distance. Street lights were to the most part non-existent out in the country, but she was pretty sure that was Sam. She walked quickly in his direction as he stepped uncertainly toward her.

"You should come back home, May - - Oh. Lila. - I thought - " He stood there, his arms at his sides, staring at her. Had she heard him correctly?

"Hey, Sam. What're you up to out here?" Lila took his arm and turned him toward his house. He had on a heavy flannel shirt, but still it wasn't enough protection against the cooling evening air. A feeling of tenderness for this good man swept over her, even as she felt a twinge of worry for him.

"Well, now, I'm not too sure. I must have dozed off in my chair and then stepped outside, and now here I am."

She looked up at him, his kind features indistinct in the dark. "And what did you have for dinner?"

"Dinner? Why in the world are you asking me about what I've eaten?"

"Just a thought. An idea that's crossed my mind lately."

"Well, now, I don't quite – oh, wait, a fine big yam from this year's crop, and a couple slices of zucchini bread. But why you would ask me about that I don't -"

"Let's get you inside. I think we've both had a pretty big evening and we're poor working stiffs who have to get up tomorrow morning." Lila opened his door and waited while he stepped inside. "Are you going to be all right?"

He lifted his head, looking much more like the Sam she knew. "All right? Of course, of course - I think I'll have a warm glass of cider and head up to bed. You need to get home yourself."

"That's exactly my plan. See you tomorrow at school." The thought of the next day made Lila wonder if moments of confusion like this had occurred at school. It was difficult enough to arrive as the new guy in charge without your staff doubting whether you had it all together.

He nodded and closed the door. Lila watched as he stood there for a moment and then walked slowly through his kitchen, turning out the light as he left the room.

# CHAPTER ELEVEN

Finally it was the end of the week, which several teachers marked by meeting for lunch in the room devoted to Family and Consumer Science: in less enlightened times, home economics. Joyce Ronley opened her low-fat blueberry yogurt container with a sigh, desire in her eyes as she watched Mary Ann Himmelstein unwrap a thick roast beef sandwich. Besides being the mother of four boys, Mary Ann's long-distance running meant she could consume anything on the planet without consequence, whereas Joyce struggled to even maintain her Rubenesque shape.

"I swear, Mary Ann, if I didn't like you so much, I'd hate you." Joyce took an emphatic bite of her carrot stick.

Eleanor Buckley, whose room this was, brought over her warmed soup from the classroom microwave. "I must say, food can certainly bring out the emotions." She was comfortably built, with soft graying hair and kind eyes. Lila could never figure out how this grandmotherly figure controlled a room full of kids, sharp objects, and hot ovens, but she did, and with great success.

Lila opened her plastic container of chicken salad, purposely small to make up for last night's dinner with Niko. "Oh yeah, it's a treacherous territory of guilt, gluttony, and denial. Look at the kids we teach — so many of them are seriously overweight, and they're in their teens! I can't imagine what will happen to their health when they get to be our age."

"But that's mostly due to just lack of knowledge, and cultural habits. Not to mention the fact that fresh vegetables aren't exactly sprouting from the sidewalks here in the city," said Joyce.

"True. It's not so easy to shop at a grocery store if you have to take two busses to get there and then carry it all back in your arms," agreed Mary Ann.

Eleanor paused, spoon in hand. "Wouldn't it be great if we could start a community garden? I should look for an empty lot near the school."

"If we ever did manage to get that off the ground, Sam Fielding's your guy. You should see what he turns out of his garden. Although sometimes I wonder if he's gone overboard. He became a strict vegan after his wife died and I'm not sure a diet like that is healthy," said Lila.

"I have no problem with vegan diets," said Eleanor, "except you need to be sure you get enough B-12. A B-12 deficiency can sneak up on you if you're not careful."

Lila looked up sharply from her salad. "What do you mean, Eleanor? How would anyone know they have a deficiency?"

Eleanor stared for a moment across the classroom. "Let's see. I think it can begin with a numbness or tingling in the hands and feet. Like you might find yourself dropping a dish, but we all do that sometimes, so it's easy to overlook. Then you might be a little unsteady on your feet and you could even have some moments of confusion. As I said, you'd probably dismiss it at first."

Eleanor had Lila's full attention now. "So how do you solve this?

What should a person with these symptoms do?"

"Plant foods have no B-12 to speak of, so the best source is liver, but it's unlikely a vegan will sit down to a big plate of that, so eggs and dairy products are your next bet. If the person still won't go that route, fortified breakfast cereals would probably do the trick. I must say you've certainly embraced this topic."

"Must be your mesmerizing skills as a teacher, Eleanor." Lila re-wrapped her uneaten cookies, put them in her lunch bag along with her salad container and stood up.

"Gotta go. I have an errand to run before the next class. Bye ladies."

Fortunately, the consumer science room, while on the third floor, was directly over the school kitchen in the basement, so it was a relatively quick trip down the four flights of stairs. Lila found the head of the school lunch program in her office. Nahiomi, in her kitchen uniform, hairnet in place, looked up from her desk. "Hi, Ms. Wallace. I was just finishing up some orders for next week. What can I do for you?"

"I'm wondering if you could do me a favor. I'm concerned that Mr. Fielding is so busy up there in the main office that he's just not eating right. He won't eat meat, but I saw that today's lunch featured vanilla custard. Do you think that you could sneak some onto his desk? Maybe tell him you need an opinion on whether the kids will like it or not?"

"Sure, that man's too skinny anyway. And next week I was going to put a cheese quiche in the breakfast program. I bet I could persuade him to try that, too."

"You're the best, Nahiomi. Just make sure he thinks it's something necessary for the school. He's kind of strict with himself when it comes to food, but he'll be on board if he thinks it's for the kids."

"I know. He's only been here a little while, but you can tell he cares about doing what's right for this place."

Suddenly they could hear the sound of a commotion in the cafeteria, where the third lunch period was finishing up. Lila stepped out of the office in time to see Coach Cleary and Bill Moynihan pulling Terrance and Leonard apart. Chairs were overturned and the other kids in the cafeteria had stopped eating to watch the show, some of them even standing on the tables to get a better view. The usual roar of conversation had swelled to an excited pandemonium. It looked as though the Terrance and Leonard feud was still in force. Anthony Paschetti was conspicuously absent, but the other assistant principal, Maritza Conception, quickly appeared, walkie-talkie in one hand, the other hand on her rounded belly.

Lila watched as the two men helped Conception escort the boys out of the cafeteria and presumably off to the office.

Later, Lila was out in the hall as usual greeting her next class and chatting with Moynihan, learning the outcome of the noon-time scuffle.

"Mr. Fielding suspended them both for four days, although they'll finish today in the in-house suspension room. I'm glad I don't have that duty. Funny how they send two kids who just had a fight to sit together in the same room," said Bill.

"True. I wouldn't want to be the in-house teacher either, but Julius Bookman somehow manages to keep them all in line," said Lila.

"The fact that he's six foot four and two hundred and fifty pounds of granite probably doesn't hurt, either."

At this the fire alarm suddenly sounded. The students in Lila's class came rushing out of the room, smiles across their faces at the thought of a shortened class period.

She called out as they went by, "Okay, slow down. Go down the stairs and out the door at the bottom of the stairs. And remember, come find me out there and I'll give you five extra points on the next test." Lila had discovered long ago that this was the most effective way of taking attendance during a fire drill, when kids really wanted to just wander off and look for their friends.

She went back into her room to grab her purse and grade book, meeting Bill again as they reached to top of the staircase. "Were we scheduled for a fire drill, Bill?"

"Not that I know of. This could actually be the real thing."

As it turned out, that was exactly what it was; someone had started a fire in a boy's room trash barrel. It was fortunate that the afternoon sun helped to warm the parking lot since the entire school had to wait outside for the fire department to arrive, find the fire, and extinguish it. At last the all-clear bell sounded and the students re-entered the building. Lila knew her students would take their sweet time returning to her class so she stayed by the inner double door leading to the exit, holding it open to speed up the process.

Paschetti, with his beloved walkie-talkie, passed through and positioned himself a short distance away, barking at the students to get to class. At the other end of the hall, Lila spotted Leonard coming towards her, traveling against the flow of bodies like a salmon swimming upstream.

His face was a study in rage and he pounded a locker with the side of one fist as he passed it.

Well, at least Paschetti was right there and would deal with him. But no, it was not to be. Unaware that anyone was watching, he took one look at Leonard, turned neatly on one heel and headed off in the opposite direction. Lila called, "Leonard!" but the angry student brushed past her and out to the street.

Later, when Lila recounted the event to Bill Moynihan, he laughed. "Paschetti might not have been very eager to confront Leonard, but he's been pretty busy this afternoon telling everyone about the non-working fire extinguisher the fire department found and what a shame it is that Mr. Fielding hadn't had them all checked."

"What? Oh, please. Sam can't be blamed for that. He's only been here a week. That Paschetti is poisonous."

"I know it pays to watch your back around him. My friend Barbara at his last school learned that."

"You mean the one he and Mrs. Galaska were at?"

"Yeah, my friend was chair of the math department there until Paschetti decided he wanted the job. After a whisper campaign that Barb was past her prime, and some book orders for the department that got mysteriously mislaid, he got himself voted in.

"I'd heard something to that effect and I've gotta say I'm not surprised."

\*\*\*

After school Lila sat at her desk, grading the last of the day's quizzes. As she entered them into her on-line grade book, she glanced over the top of her computer down the quiet hallway outside her room. Stella Slocumb was leaning against the wall, head down, holding a notebook against her chest. She appeared to be crying. Lila started to push back her chair and see what the matter was but at that moment Ty Harkasian came down the hall and stopped, speaking quietly with her. Stella shook her head, her long brown ponytail swinging. Harkasian spoke some more, touching the girl's shoulder briefly, and Stella looked up at him with a watery smile. They parted, going in opposite directions, but when the handsome young teacher passed her door, Lila thought he looked worried.

# CHAPTER TWELVE

"Niko? Is that you? What are you doing back here?" The tall dried grass rustled against her jeans as she cut across the field, walking as though through deep water, shading her eyes from the late afternoon sun with her hand. She had decided to take a walk before dinner to empty her mind of school.

Niko spun away from the other man with him who was holding a mallet and a fistful of orange-tipped stakes. Her neighbor stepped in front of his companion as Lila approached.

"I think this is Sam's land back here. Doesn't yours end over by that oak? I remember walking it with him last month."

"Lila! I was just showing my friend Jorge the old rail tracks at the end of our properties."

Jorge quietly smiled and nodded, transferring stakes and mallet to the other hand, moving them down to his side, out of Lila's view.

"Lila is quite the good neighbor, Jorge. Looking out for everyone's interests." His smile stopped at his mouth as his eyes darted involuntarily to Jorge, then the stakes, then back to Lila.

"Does Sam know you're out here?"

Niko stepped forward again, taking her by the elbow and leaning conspiratorially toward her. "It is not to worry; I chatted with Sam on my way. Now how can I persuade you to take such a keen interest in my land, too?"

She found she was being steered skillfully back to Niko's adjoining field, the mysterious Jorge several yards behind them.

"Well, I think good neighbors always look out for each other," she said, hating herself for this bromide.

"And is that what we are? Good neighbors?" She glanced over as he tilted his head and raised his eyebrows. How on earth could anyone have such ridiculously long eyelashes, she thought? She kept her chin up and her focus resolutely ahead, avoiding those pools of dusk trained on her. Sidestepping this possible conversational minefield, she said, "Looking out for each other's interests is just part of small town living. And since Sam and I have known each other for so long, what concerns one of us concerns the other."

Still ignoring the presence of Jorge, only a few yards away, Niko leaned closer, "Then I must attempt to also become someone about whom you are 'concerned.'"

This was supposed to have been a walk to clear her mind, not fill it up with new conundrums. "I should be getting back. Have a nice evening." With a nod to Niko and Jorge – who was he anyway? – she turned away, narrowly dodging a boulder in front of her.

She reached the end of the field and cut through a short patch of pines, probably planted as a wind brake by a long-ago farmer. It soon opened to another clearing and before she had much time to ponder her meeting with Niko, she came upon Sam in his pumpkin field. What had started as a solitary hike had turned into quite the social event, she thought to herself. He appeared to be harvesting late pumpkins, and had a heap of at least ten of all shapes and sizes at the edge of the field. Straightening up, he spotted her and smiled.

"Lila! What a pleasant surprise. How'd you like a pumpkin for your front porch, or maybe your classroom? I still seem to have a few left and I thought I might as well bring them into school - bring in a little country for the city kids to enjoy. "

"Hi, Sam. What a nice thought. A small one to put on my desk would be fun."

"Well, go dig in the pile over there and see which one suits your fancy. I'm leaving some in the fields as food for the squirrels and rabbits and to start next year's crop, but there are still a few good ones there."

The mention of school triggered a thought in her head and as she sorted through the pumpkins she glanced up at him. "Some of us were chatting at lunch in Eleanor Buckley's room and the subject of diets came up."

He brushed the dirt from a pumpkin, "Not too shocking, Lila, for a bunch of women eating lunch."

"No, I mean, we were talking about the effects of different diets, ways of eating. I worry that you're not getting everything you need from that vegan diet of yours and I wonder if you'd do me a favor."

He began piling pumpkins into a small garden cart. "I hope you're not going to ask me to return to my days as a heartless carnivore."

"No, but I think you'd feel a lot better if you made a habit of cereal in the morning – fortified cereal. Even good old Wheaties would do the trick if you ate them on a regular basis."

They began walking back together, Sam pushing the cart, Lila holding her pumpkin. "Well, now, if it will set your mind at ease, and I could pour some almond milk over them, I believe I could manage that." He looked down at her, smiling, his blue eyes meeting hers. She found herself returning his smile. It was growing dim out now and it was pleasant there in the fading light.

Pulling herself out of this reverie, she said, "Oh! How did I forget? Before I got to your field I found Niko and some man wandering around on your property line."

"Well, part of that line is his. I don't see how that's cause for concern."

"I don't know – they just seemed awfully shifty. Oh, and Niko had a clipboard and I could have sworn I saw stakes like the ones you mark property with."

"A clipboard! The cad! The bounder!" His grin widened. "I imagine a number of stakes have become dislodged over the years. He was probably just replacing them."

She stubbornly refused to embrace his sunny view of the world. "I just hope that's all it was." She shifted the pumpkin in her arms. "Well, thanks for this. We'll have to part ways here; I'm heading for home. I'm looking forward to a long quiet evening on the couch."

"Good night, Lila." He reached across and gave her shoulder a quick squeeze.

He continued on with his wheelbarrow while she cut diagonally across the field toward Old County Road. She strolled along the quiet road, pondering Niko's motives and Sam's competency. It seemed that both were becoming hard to assess. She stepped to the bank of the road as a car passed her. She was conscious of her vulnerability in the growing dark.

Reaching her house, she noticed that she had left one of the windows cracked to let in the fresh afternoon air. She would need to close it now that the sun had set. Thankfully, Winston's hunting must not have been successful; there were no gifts of tiny corpses waiting by the door.

She entered the house, putting the pumpkin on the hall table and went into the dining room to close the window she had spotted. She narrowly missed stepping on the big cat where he crouched in the dark. "Winston! What are you up to?" He ignored her question, instead continuing to stare up pointedly at the window. She followed his gaze and was rewarded with the silhouette of a chipmunk scrabbling up the screen, on the inside of the window.

Sighing, she said, "You are a bad, bad cat, Winston," and after shutting the glass portion of the window, went back outside. She fought her way through the old rhododendrons next to the house. She hoped the screen wasn't firmly seated, but she was in luck. She lifted the screen two or three inches, the chipmunk riding along as the screen rose, and climbed out of the shrubbery. Instead of scampering to safety, he hung there like some sort of window decoration. She hoped he'd eventually figure out he was free, and had learned a valuable lesson about cat evasion.

Winston was now in the kitchen, looking at her reproachfully. She said to him, "I don't care. You are forbidden to bring any more friends home. Maybe I should get some proper playmates for you. How about a couple of bouncy kittens to keep you company?" Unable to voice how very repellent this idea was, he instead turned his back on her and faced his empty food bowl.

"Yes, I'm aware that it's empty and you are being horribly mistreated." Lila opened a can of cat food, emptying half into his bowl.

She next poured herself a glass of Riesling and assembled a plate of Gorgonzola and sliced apples, adding two slices of sourdough bread from the bakery for good measure. She carried her meal into the living room, picking up her laptop along the way. This old house had begun feeling more like hers each day and she was becoming curious about its past. Long ago it had just been the place where she could go to her room and close the door on annoying parents. Now it might be interesting to find out more about where she lived. She realized she didn't even know how old the house was or who had owned it before her parents.

Lila propped her feet up on the coffee table, computer in her lap, and went to the Calvin town website, scanning her choices until she found the Historical Commission link. Once there, she entered her street address and called up the information. It seemed her house had been built in 1905 as the farmhouse for Maymie and Noah Morris, who represented the third generation of a prominent family in the area. It had later been sold in the 1940s to William Graves who had resided there until it changed hands once more, into the possession of her parents. Well, that was easily researched, she thought. She wondered what else the website might divulge. She remembered Niko and his friend with the property markers.

She wandered about for a bit through the departments, Animal Control, Conservation, Library, Park and Recreation, Planning . . .Planning and Community Development – that was the one. She clicked on the link and found herself looking at the agenda for a meeting scheduled in three weeks. The purpose appeared to be to provide an opportunity for the public to weigh in on amendments to the town's zoning bylaws. The items in question involved unregistered motor vehicles, solar energy systems, and the district's flood plane. Much more interesting was a request regarding the procedures for transferring the designation of land from agricultural to commercial use. Could this have anything to do with Niko's business park?

She turned off her laptop and put it on the other side of Winston, who had wedged himself into the spot next to her. She told herself she would not get worked up until she knew more. But did Niko really plan to chop up good farm land, Calvin's diminishing open space, for fields of asphalt and concrete buildings?

It was getting late. If she was going to relax enough to sleep tonight she needed to empty her head of land schemes and wheeling and dealing. She picked up the soothingly mindless murder mystery she had begun. What she needed at the moment was a whodunit someone else would solve. She had been a wash-out so far in divining what Niko was up to, or what his friend Jorge was doing there. And Anthony Paschetti was difficult to figure out, too. She had a feeling that whatever he had something up his sleeve wasn't good. It had been a long day and the only mysterious men she felt capable of dealing with right now were fictional ones. She settled lengthwise on the couch, pulled the old family quilt from its back and draped it over her legs. Winston claimed the valley between the couch back and her legs, and began washing.

"You are still a stubborn, untrainable boy, but at least you're easy to read, unlike the other men in my life."

# CHAPTER THIRTEEN

Early Monday morning Lila was just fitting her key into her classroom door while juggling both a pumpkin and her cup of tea when she heard steps. She looked around to find a somewhat breathless Stella Slocumb at her side. The girl appeared to be near tears, her heavy eye make-up already smudging under her lashes.

"Stella? What are you doing here so early? Did you have a pass from someone to get in before school opens?"

The girl shook her head. Her dark hair had been carefully sculpted to drape seductively across half of her face, but Lila could still see the worry written there. She pushed the door open and held it. "Come on in. Let me just put my things down and we'll have a chat."

The sun hadn't finished its ascent for the day and the room lights felt harsh after the relative darkness of the hallways. Lila piled her belongings on the long counter under the big classroom windows and turned to Stella as she took off her coat. "Does this have anything to do with the essay? It's not due till the end of the week."

Stella dumped her heavy backpack on the floor and dropped gracelessly into one of the student desks in the front row. "No." Head down, knees together, feet on either side of the desk chair, she resembled a sulky child, or at least a child in black patterned hose and an eight-inch skirt. She didn't meet Lila's eye and traced the carving on the desk with a deeply purple fingernail.

Sitting on the corner of her big teacher's desk, concerned but exasperated, Lila said, "Why are you here, Stella? What can I do for you?"

"Oh, Miss. I don't know what to do." As Stella lifted her face a black tear rolled down it.

Lila automatically offered the ever-present box of classroom tissues and moved to the student desk next to the girl. "What is it, sweetie? Tell me what the matter is."

All in one breath, Stella said, "I guess I didn't believe it would happen to me just other girls and it was just that once, well maybe twice, and my mother's going to kill me, especially after what happened with my sister and how am I going to finish the year and I think I'm going to throw up."

Lila crossed the room, returning with the trashcan. She put her hand on the girl's arm. "Are you pregnant, Stella?"

"Shit yes. I mean, I'm sorry, Miss. It's been like a month or more and I took one of those tests, and then another and I'm sick in the morning and all I do is pee."

"Does the father know?"

Stella snorted. "My dad? Not likely, we haven't seen him for over a year."

"No, Stella. The father of the baby. It took two of you to accomplish this. You

shouldn't be dealing with this on your own. He bears as much
responsibility as you."

"No, I haven't told him. I haven't told anyone. I don't know where to
start. I guess I wanted to just pretend like all this wasn't happening."

"How about we start with Mrs. Li down in Guidance? Would you feel
comfortable talking with her?"

"I guess. She's okay." Stella looked up anxiously. "She won't tell
anyone, will she?"

"Not unless you want her to. But she knows resources I may not and
she could help you with scheduling if we need to change your classes or
plan time out of school. Here, let me write you a pass and you can go right
there before school starts."

Stella took in several shuddering breaths and began to gather up her
things.

Lila handed her the pass along with more tissues. Putting her arm
around Stella's shoulders, she walked the girl to the door. "I'll give her a call
right now to tell her you're on your way. She's really very nice, but let me
know how your meeting with her goes, okay?"

"Okay. Thanks, Miss." Stella attempted a wan smile and trudged
slowly in the direction of the school's main office.

Poor kid. Lila turned back to her room and began organizing for the
day, her mind still on Stella and how the girl's life had just taken a sudden
turn. Sadly, this wasn't the first time she'd had a conversation like this with
one of her students. And they'd become more frequent over the years. It
was ironic that birth control was more available now than ever before but

this still kept happening. What a shame. Stella wasn't that strong academically, but Lila had heard that she showed real promise in art class, maybe even had a shot at a scholarship to art school.

Lila's morning went by quickly, filled with poetry and the effort of pulling kids through it, trying to help them see how different it was from prose, how much could be said with so few words. At her door, in between classes, she spotted Stella coming up the stairs, looking decidedly more cheerful. The meeting with Ramona Li in guidance must have gone well, or maybe it was just the resilience of youth. Stella's face brightened further as Ty Harkasian started down the staircase toward her. Ignoring the traffic working its way around her, she stopped on the landing to speak with the handsome young teacher, leaning on the heavy metal railing. Suddenly it pulled from the wall, sending Stella's books flying and leaving her teetering on the edge of the stair. Lila watched as Ty stepped quickly across the landing, putting a hand to the girl's shoulder to steady her. Anthony Paschetti was just coming up the stairs and Lila could have sworn he looked almost pleased at the scene.

"Shouldn't you be heading to class, young lady, not loitering here on the stairs?" To Ty he said, "Looks like the building is falling apart, lately, doesn't it, Mr. Harkasian? Someone should be seeing to this maintenance, although I doubt if our new principal has thought of it." He continued up to the third floor and came to a stop by Lila. "Did you see that, Ms Wallace? A lawsuit waiting to happen. I wonder if Mr. Fielding realizes the risks of poor building management. I mean, don't get me wrong. Believe me, I know how hard it is to stay on top of everything in a school of this size. Fielding is trying his best, I'm sure, but not everyone has what it takes."

He reminded Lila of a carrier pigeon somehow. Maybe it was that beaky nose and the way he puffed out his chest when he spoke, or perhaps his delight in delivering news – as long as it was negative. She opened her mouth in rebuttal and then thought better of it. She turned on her heel and just went into her room, leaving him standing alone in the emptying hallway.

Climbing back upstairs from the basement mailroom that afternoon, Lila decided to look in on Sam and warn him about the broken railing from the morning. She had called the custodian to forestall any more mishaps, but she thought he needed to be ready for future insinuations by Paschetti. The main office was busy with parents waiting for their students, students waiting to call parents, teachers bustling in and out, and ringing phones. Lila waved to Tiana as she passed by, pointing to Sam's office to indicate her purpose there. A student was standing at the secretary's desk, arguing in Spanish on the phone while Tiana printed out a bus route from her computer for a parent waiting impatiently at the long front counter.

Sam was at his desk, staring intently at his computer, a spoon in one hand and a dish of vanilla custard in the other. He glanced over as she entered. "Hi, Lila. Do you have any idea how many emails I receive from Central Office alone each day? It's a wonder anyone gets anything done in this system. When we're not in some interminable meeting we seem to spend all our time writing and reading emails. I guess I had forgotten about the joys of administration during those couple of years off the job."

"I didn't want to interrupt your lunch. I just wanted to give you a heads-up about the railing on the third floor stairs by my room."

He pulled his eyes from the screen and smiled at her, "Lunch is a forgotten luxury lately; I just grab what I can. And yes, Mr. Paschetti has preceded you. I'm well aware of the event."

"Paschetti is a busy guy; it's hard to find time to spread all that bad news. On a happier note, it looks like Nahiomi from the cafeteria is taking good care of you." She pointed to the now-empty custard cup.

"Yes, I have to say, if she didn't put this food right in front of me I'd probably forget to eat. I felt I could relax my principles a little since she was kind enough to bring it to me personally. And of course eating dairy products doesn't involve killing innocent animals. "

"That's very true. I'd better get going, though. I have hall duty in a few minutes." As Lila turned to leave, Joyce Ronley appeared in the doorway, with freshly applied lipstick, a flattering deep indigo dress, and a pie.

"Hi Lila, I see you're leaving. I just stopped by to ask Mr. Fielding if he'd be willing to test this pumpkin and pecan pie I'm experimenting with." Smiling, she placed the pan on his desk as he looked up at her. Hall duty forgotten, Lila halted in her tracks and watched. Was Joyce actually batting her eyelashes? And what about all those emails he was just complaining about? Lila was tempted to point out to Sam that the pie had probably been made with not only milk, but several eggs.

"That's mighty thoughtful of you, Ms. Ronley, but an entire pie. . ."

"Joyce, please! And if you're brave enough to be my guinea pig, I think you've earned it." It was interesting how Joyce's ample bosom was positioned directly in Sam's line of sight as he sat at his desk. She leaned over slightly to push the pie two inches closer to him. "I'll just leave this with you. Now you be sure to let me know how you like it."

Good grief, thought Lila. From all appearances, Joyce was weaving her web for husband number three. She supposed she should hand it to her. Unlike Lila, she was unafraid to make a commitment, no matter how short.

Taking one last look at the unsuspecting Sam, leaning back in his desk chair and smiling, and Joyce, fluffing the back of her hair, Lila departed for what was now beginning to seem like a saner world in the halls of the high school. As she walked away she could hear laughter, first Joyce's, then Sam's.

# CHAPTER FOURTEEN

The next day Lila stopped in the center of town on her way home to pick up something at the village store that would be easy for dinner. According to the Calvin Historical Society plaque on its white clapboard, the Binding-Stevens building first appeared in 1820. It had been a store of some kind most of its existence: first selling small and large animal feed, then dry goods, a short period of selling gifts and antiques, then a failed French restaurant. Now it had returned, providing soup, sandwiches and a modest assortment of last-minute groceries and meals to over-extended housewives, plus Scrabble and couches for the students from the prep-school two blocks down Main Street.

She entered and inhaled the mingled odors of that day's spinach soup and the Mediterranean Quiche she had seen chalked on the blackboard outside. Her evening's menu decided, she stepped up to wait her turn at the counter. A thirty-fiveish woman with close-cropped hair and a nose stud was paying for her veggie-wrap while next in line two teenagers considered the array of oversized cookies on display in the showcase.

Idly glancing across the store, Lila spotted Niko, of all people, sitting at one of the retro tin-topped kitchen tables. With him, in a cloud of blond hair and deep discussion, was Arlene Gerrigan. The table was blanketed in papers, some of which looked to be land surveys. Niko appeared busy, alternatively poring over the papers and picking up items from the floor as they were scattered by Arlene's over-caffeinated gestures on the other side of the table. Lifting his head, his eye caught Lila's and he began tidying the materials. Meanwhile, Arlene dropped in succession her glasses, her phone, and two pens. Her possessions finally restored, and papers stowed in her briefcase, the two rose and shook hands.

The teenagers before Lila finally reached a decision about the cookies. Behind the counter Libby began placing the kids' choices in a bag as Niko materialized at Lila's elbow.

"Lila. What an unexpected and delightful surprise," he murmured in her ear.

She took an involuntary step away, "Hi Niko. Fancy meeting you here." She looked pointedly at the realtor as she exited, phone to her ear, real estate listings trailing from her briefcase. She wondered if he would explain what he and Arlene had been up to.

"Yes." He said, "A happy coincidence." No, thought Lila, apparently no explanation would be provided. He continued, "Now that we have met so fortuitously, perhaps I could prevail upon you to join me this evening?"

"Oh, gee, I don't know Niko. It's been a long day and. . ."

"Not even for a drive? People have been telling me of a particularly scenic spot, and it would be so helpful if, as a native of this town, you could assist me in finding it." Blond eyebrows raised innocently, Niko seemed to be doing his best to look earnest rather than predatory. Stalling for time, Lila gave her dinner order and then turned back to him. Why not, she thought. After what she had witnessed with Sam and Joyce that afternoon, perhaps it wouldn't be such a bad idea. Sam sure didn't seem to mind stopping his day to be plied with baked goods. No reason why she shouldn't take a simple drive to help out a neighbor. At the very least, she might be able to pry some information out of this Greek clam about what he and Arlene had been cooking up. "Yes, I think I have time for a short drive. Why don't you pick me up in an hour and a half?"

Perfect white teeth on display, Niko said, "Wonderful! I will see you then." She had the feeling that, given a chance, he would have bowed over her hand. Instead, he paused to smile meaningfully at her and then he departed through the store entrance with the stride of a victorious general.

Her dinner riding next to her on the passenger seat, she turned from Main onto Old County. Before she could reach her driveway, she had to stop in the road for a procession of wild turkey hens as they crossed. Some members of the group were somewhat smaller, probably teenagers who had hatched earlier in the year. To kill time, she counted them as they paraded in front of her car – fifteen, no, here came one more, sixteen. There were no males; they'd appear in the spring to perform their kabuki dance of love for their future mates, puffing themselves up and displaying their tail feathers. Now there's an analogy, she thought, finally pulling up at her house. It brought to mind the marked differences between Niko and Sam, one like a bright-feathered tom with his sports cars and enigmatic behavior, the other clothed in flannel shirts and uncomplicated honesty.

She walked back to pick up the mail from the roadside mailbox, sorting through the magazines and flyers as she returned. Tucking them under her arm, she shifted the bag holding her dinner to the other hand so she could unlock the door. Winston sat waiting in the hall, a dead mouse at his feet.

"Finally! Now you've got it! This is what you're supposed to be doing around here. I can't say my favorite thing is to scrape up dead mice as soon as I get in the door, but it's good to know you're on the job." Winston sniffed at the mouse and then began washing one paw as if to say, this was nothing, just another day in the life of a superior hunter.

After dealing with the mouse and heating her dinner, Lila relaxed and watched the news as she ate. She left a corner of her quiche on the plate and lowered it to the floor for the cat lounging on the rug. "There's your reward, big fella. Keep up the good work. It's fall and we're going to have plenty of mice hoping to join us for the winter."

Niko would be there soon; she'd already changed into her jeans, but her hair could use some work. She gave it a good brushing and wrestled it into a ponytail. She had heard that women's hair often thinned as they grew older; she reflected that in her case that might be something to look forward to. She was digging her white fleece jacket from the hall closet as a low-throated roar sounded outside. Peering out the window, she saw a very impractical vehicle pulling up in back of her own car. Whatever scenic spot Niko had in mind had better have good roads leading to it. She'd eat her hat if that car was any more than eight inches off the ground.

As it turned out, the red sports car was perfect for a slow twilight ride down country roads. She was doubtful when they drove off with the top still down, but sitting deep in the bucket seat with the warm air from the heater flowing over her, it began to make perfect sense. Three dignified llamas gazed over the fence of the Dziobek farm as they drove up Calvin Mountain. The windows of the farm's pre-revolutionary homestead glowed golden in the growing dark, and Lila could see Roberta Dziobek on her way back from the barn, probably after feeding the chickens.

Farms were becoming a rarity in the area, and the next buildings they passed were more typical of contemporary Calvin. McMansions, some of the townies called them, but although they sat on large swaths of verdant farmland, the owners of these massive homes never got close to the land except when riding around on their lawn tractors -- assuming they even did their own yard work. Stone walls lined much of the road; they were probably two hundred years old but were still in such good shape that Lila found it hard to see over some of them from her seat in the low-slung car.

"So where are we going? You seem to be finding your way just fine without my help."

"I confess I did acquire directions from Arlene at the store this afternoon. I had learned that this place called Indian Point commands a view of the entire valley. Have you seen it?

Good grief. Of course she'd seen it. Any teenager in town with romance in his soul had been there at some time or other. At least on a Tuesday evening there would be less chance of encountering rows of cars with steamed windows.

"Yeees. But it will be too dark by the time we get there to see much of anything." She was sure this did not bode well for a low-key evening.

"That is true, but I expect the city lights will provide a dramatic sight."

At this he turned the car onto Hilltop Road, which was paved, but it was so narrow two cars would find it challenging to pass abreast. In the summer the trees met overhead, but with the leaves now almost gone, looking up, she could see stars through the branches. At the end of the road was the fire tower, which had been re-purposed as a cell tower by the town fire department. There was also a clearing for utility trucks, but used more often for other, far less official, purposes. Niko pulled up to the low fence, and turned off the engine. The silence felt sudden after the constant muffled roar of the car, and it was all the more pleasurable because of it. They sat there without speaking for several minutes, the only sound the rustlings in the nearby woods of small animals who must have decided Niko and Lila posed no threat. He turned toward her, putting his hand on the top of her seat.

"Have you always lived in this town?"

She continued to look over the lights of the valley below. "I grew up here but went to college in Washington D.C. and stayed there afterwards. Teaching in the city schools was good practice for my work at Thomas Paine."

"Washington is such an exciting place. What brought you back?"

"My parents. My mother's health wasn't very strong and she had found it difficult to care for my father when he was diagnosed with colon cancer. It was a hard time; they were so close. I think that's when I really got to know Sam since he had similar challenges with his wife's illness."

"And both of your parents are no longer with you?"

"No. They died in the same year. It seemed odd at first to be living here without them. Something about returning to your childhood home makes you forget that you're all grown up."

It occurred to Lila that this was not going at all the way she had planned. Like previous conversations with Niko, the exchange of information was completely one-sided so far. "So you and Arlene looked very busy this afternoon. What were you up to?" There, she thought. The direct approach.

He tilted his head as he answered, leaning just a bit closer. "Oh, I was just satisfying my curiosity about your wonderful town. There is so much to learn when you find yourself in a new place. Don't you agree?"

She thought she could feel his hand playing lightly with her ponytail and although she turned toward him, she now had her back against the car door, in a effort to increase the distance between them. "So are you looking for something in particular, Niko?" Damn, she hadn't meant that to sound so suggestive.

Smiling, Niko moved still closer, his hand now firmly at the back of her head. "I was not, but I had told myself I would know it when I saw it . . . ."

His lips grazed hers but she pulled back into the remaining few inches of the car she had left. "I think it's time we get back, Niko."

He stayed where he was, still smiling, his hand still behind her head. After a beat, his smile widened and he sat back, refastening his seat belt. "As you wish." And they drove slowly back down the mountain to the quiet town below.

# CHAPTER FIFTEEN

Friday morning Lila knocked on the door of the classroom for in-house suspension. It was, by necessity, locked. Otherwise, friends of the incarcerated tended to horse around by opening the door and yelling in comments. As it was, the patience of the teacher, Julius Bookman, was often tested by poundings of passersby and rattlings of the doorknob. At the sound of Lila's rap, Mr. Bookman himself responded, his massive frame filling the doorway. She was reminded of a large household appliance. In the hushed room behind him, students sat in various attitudes, resentment and boredom dominating. One girl appeared to be asleep, but most of the other kids looked up at this break in the monotony.

She was there to drop off the work she'd gathered for her charming but wayward student, Trevor, who was sitting near the door. He had been the catalyst for the latest food fight in the cafeteria. Apparently undaunted by the prospect of a full day of silent labor, he smiled sweetly at her as she handed him the assignment. She doubted if she'd ever see it again, but at least she had tried.

Now it was time to get to her hall duty. She closed the classroom door behind her and glanced down the hallway where she was surprised to see Assistant Superintendent Margaret Daniele and Maritza Concepcion standing together outside Maritza's office. Assistant superintendents didn't usually drop by on social calls. They both appeared to be smiling, but ended their conversation when Lila reached them.

Coming up to them, Lila said, "Hi Margaret. How nice to see you again."

"Hey Lila. You, too. Looks like life here at Thomas Paine has settled to an even keel with Mr. Fielding at its helm."

"I couldn't agree more," said Maritza. "And he's a pleasure to work with."

"Yeah, thanks for talking him into the job, Margaret."

"No, we were lucky to get him. It was great he was willing to come out of retirement. Not too many people of his caliber around. Present company excepted." With this last comment, Daniele smiled meaningfully at Concepcion.

"Aw, shucks, Ms. Daniele," said Maritza. "You'll make me blush."

Lila continued smiling, unsure about the turn the conversation had taken. Something appeared to be in the works, but it looked like she'd have to wait to find out exactly what.

"I'll give you a call in a few days to see what you've decided. That is, if that baby hasn't decided to arrive early!" Daniele departed down the hall, waving a goodbye over her shoulder.

"Well, I'd better get going myself." Lila turned, passing Anthony Paschetti who was standing in the middle of the staircase to the second floor. Had he been there the whole time? Who knew, she thought. The man always seemed to be lurking and listening around corners lately, particularly in the vicinity of anyone with power. .

Now at her post by the second floor back stairway, she watched as the hallway rush thinned down to the students who were too cool or too careless to worry about getting to class on time. She reflected that hall duty wasn't all that different from being a fireman; periods of dull boredom punctuated by sudden moments of excitement. If only today would be one of the quiet ones. She had hopes of writing a test on Emily Dickinson for next week.

Two big boys ambled by, laughing, as one pounded the other's arm and the other did a body-block in response, neither showing any signs of concern over tardiness or even recognition that she was there. Speeding around the corner and overtaking them came M&M, carrying a loose-leaf notebook. Chagrin washed over their faces as Miss O'Shaughnessy halted their progress, separated them, handed the notebook to the larger of the two, and walked him to a nearby classroom. Lila was reminded of a herd of sheep being maneuvered by a diminutive border collie. The second student turned on his heel and headed up the staircase to his class. Maura Mary smiled at Lila as she exited the classroom, "That Keshawn would forget his head if it wasn't nailed on," and continued down the hall, onto her next mission. Lila wondered if she'd ever have even a portion of the energy M&M expended in a day.

Two girls came up the staircase from the first floor, but she recognized them as helpers from the guidance department, and sure enough, they brought their hall passes over for her to see, not even waiting for her to request them. She waved them on their way as Mrs. Concepcion approached from the right.

"Hello again, Miss Wallace. How things with you this morning?" The administrator stopped by her side, smiling.

"Just fine, Mrs. Concepcion. And how are you doing, or are you sick and tired of people asking you that?" Maritza Concepcion looked as though her maternity leave should start next week, not the projected date of a month away.

"Oh, fine. I'm learning to pace myself. Thought I'd do a few spins through the halls while I've got my morning energy still with me."

Ty Harkasian went by, jogging up the stairs from the first to the third floor, his arms full of papers, apparently on his way back from the copier.

"There's your poster boy for energy. Oh, to be twenty-five again."

"Lila, speaking of Ty, have you noticed anything with him lately?"

"What do you mean?"

"Well, I don't mean to single him out. But I have spotted him with Stella Slocomb on more than one occasion. Maybe I'm just being over-cautious."

Lila was taken aback. Was Maritza suggesting that Ty was acting inappropriately with a student? "Stella's going through a rough patch right now. And Ty may be young – and ridiculously good-looking – but he's a sensible guy. I think he's just trying to help her, give her an understanding ear."

"I hope you're right and I'm just being a worry-wart. Forget I said anything. I'd better go. One more turn through the hall and I'm back to my office. I have a parent coming in soon."

The assistant principal walked off, slowing a jogging student to a walk with an upraised hand, and then she disappeared around the next corner. Lila verified the student's pass, sent him on his way, and then settled herself at the student desk left in the hall for teachers on duty. She took out her papers to prepare the test but the memory of Ty and Stella talking, their heads close, flashed in her mind.

The morning classes behind her, Lila closed her classroom door, cleared a space on her desk, and pulled out her lunch. She was opening her salad dressing as Bill Moynihan stuck his head in her room. "Mind if I join you? You don't even have to talk to me. I just need to be in the presence of another adult for a few minutes."

"Hi Bill. Come on in. I know exactly what you mean. It's been a long morning."

They worked their way through sandwich and salad, comparing the successes and frustrations of their morning.

" - and I can't help it," said Bill. "I still wish kids had their times tables drilled into them in middle school like the good old days. When they arrive without even the basics, it makes everything else take so much longer."

"I feel your pain. It's a real challenge to discuss author technique when your students can't even recognize an adjective."

The door to her classroom opened and they looked up to see Ty Harkasian entered. "Hi Lila, Hi Bill. How's it going?"

Bill Moynihan glanced at the clock and quickly gathered up the debris from his lunch. "Hey, Ty. I hate to eat and run, but I have a kid coming by to make up a quiz before the next class."

Ty sat at the student desk closest to Lila's as Bill exited the room. "Lila, have you got a minute?"

"Sure. If my clock is correct, I even have six."

He sat looking at her for a moment; he seemed to be considering how to begin. "What is it?" she asked. "Is something the matter?"

"No. Nothing specific. I mean, I was talking to Paschetti the other day – "

"Well, there's your first mistake," Lila closed the lid to her plastic salad container with a snap.

"I know. He can be a real piece of work. But, I mean, how well do you know Mr. Fielding? I mean, what do you know about him? Is he okay?"

Ty was a good guy, but Lila could feel her eyes narrowing and her defenses kicking into gear. "What do you mean? Okay how?"

"Well, I know he was the principal in Calvin for years, but that's a small town. Paschetti doesn't seem to think Fielding can handle a school like ours – you know, in the city."

"Well, first of all, you need to take everything Paschetti says with a grain of salt – or maybe a whole truckload. He's convinced his destiny is to become principal here, and I'm beginning to wonder what he'd be willing to do to make that happen. And secondly, are you aware of the number of fights that *didn't* happen because Sam just somehow was there and caught it before things got messy? I think he can handle an inner-city school just fine. The kids are actually listening to him, which is more than I can say about

Paschetti. I've seen them laugh at him as he goes by."

"No, you're right. I don't know why I listen to the guy. But you should know that he's also saying the funds from the school fundraiser are misplaced – he's saying they were in Sam's office."

"What? Oh please. I'm sure that's all they are – misplaced. And now I should get ready for my next class." She took a sip from her iced tea and tucked her padded lunch bag back into a drawer in her desk.

"Wait, there's one more thing I'd like to run by you. You've been teaching a little longer than I have – how should I handle personal information from a student? One of my kids has gotten herself into a jam and I want to help, but I don't want to betray a confidence."

"Can you tell me who it is?"

"I guess. Maybe you already know what's going on. You have her for a student, too. It's Stella."

"Yeah. I sent her on to Ramona down in Guidance. I'm hoping it was helpful. You know Stella's pregnant, right?"

"Yes, she told me the other day. I wanted to send her to the nurse when she left in the middle of class and told me after that she'd been sick. She explained it happens to her a lot now in the morning and I guessed the rest."

"It's too bad. Stella's not exactly Rhodes Scholar material, but just a little more effort and she'd have a good shot at college – particularly an art school from what I hear of her work. I hate to see some of our girls' futures shift like that. Any idea who the father is?" She looked sharply at him, remembering her earlier conversation with Maritza.

"I couldn't say. She's a member of my church and she was at the last retreat, so I got to know her last summer. I just hope it all works out. She's a little flaky, but she's a good kid."

"She is. It's too bad. Well, I guess all we can do is lend her a shoulder when she needs it."

At this the bell rang. "Great. Off to my favorite thing, lunch duty." He rose from the desk as Lila's door opened to the first wave of students.

"See you later, Mr. Harkasian. Hi, Sasha. Hi, Jacob. Gilberto, is this your paper? I found it after the last class, but you forgot to put your name on it-"

***

"Hey there, how's it going? Are you still eating your Wheaties?" Lila's words brought Sam's head out of the storage cupboard in his office. With one period left in the day, the main office was as busy as ever with kids being dismissed early and teachers dropping off information on club meetings and sports practices for the end of the day announcements. The principal's office was an oasis of quiet.

"Hi Lila. My Wheaties? Oh. Sure thing. Every morning like clockwork and I must admit, I think it's helped. I don't seem to be forgetting things the way I used to, but right now I could use a giant bowlful. Thought I put that envelope right here . . . " Sam's voice drifted from clear to muffled as he poked his head back into the recesses of the tall cupboard.

"What's up? You missing something?"

"Ms. O'Shaughnessy dropped off the final tally of the school fundraiser along with the money itself. I know that she stood right where you are and watched me put it in this cupboard and lock it up. I can't imagine where it's gotten to."

"And you're sure you locked it in this cupboard?" Given Sam's memory lapses, anything seemed possible.

"Absolutely. This is the key for it." He separated a key from the cluster on a ring of other keys. He closed the cupboard door and began to demonstrate locking the door. "Well, that's odd."

"What is it?"

"I don't remember this door looking quite like this."

She stepped closer to the door and stared at it with him. There were scratch marks in the metal surrounding the key hole.

"Gosh. It looks like someone forced this lock. How much money are we talking about?"

"Not a fortune, but still enough to make it worth stealing. $237. This is terrible. Everyone worked so hard on that fundraiser. Lila, I'm going to ask you to keep this quiet."

"Of course. How else can I help?'

He sighed and rubbed his forehead. This just isn't fair, she thought. He didn't deserve this. And this didn't look like a random attack by some student. For one thing, Sam was very conscientious about locking his office door and Tiana watched the main office area like a hawk. Something weird was going on. She just knew it. "Just keep your eyes and ears open. Someone may decide to exercise some bragging rights."

"Will do. For now, I'm afraid I have to get back upstairs. See you later." She gave his arm a squeeze and departed as Sam continued to stare at the scene of the crime.

She left the main office as the bell rang to release students from class. She spotted Warren and Stella, who may have cut the last class since they were already in the hall, drifting slowly together down the corridor. She wondered what they had been doing out of class. She continued up to the second floor, trying to stay ahead of the wave of humanity rushing up with her and get to her room before she was slowed down by the saunterers and foot-draggers. As she crossed the landing and began mounting the next flight to her floor she saw Mr. Paschetti by a student locker. If she didn't know better, she would have sworn he had just closed it. Yet the administration did have access to all lockers. The combination locks were built in, not brought from home, so there was a master list of all the combinations. Oh, well, who knew? Perhaps a student was absent and had left something vital at school.

One thing she was sure of, she needed to get to her room before some of the more imaginative students decided she was absent, giving them a ticket to wander the halls. Substitutes were notorious for missing names when taking attendance. Or so the kids would have her believe.

# CHAPTER SIXTEEN

Rather than succumb to her first impulse, which was to sink into her couch and never emerge, Lila decided to be noble and brave and get a jump on the weekend laundry. Not much else happening on a Friday night in her mad-cap social life, she reflected. At least her on-again, off-again dating in Washington had provided something besides school and housework. Life here in Calvin had proved to be quiet indeed. Her investigative dinners with Niko didn't count as actual dating, did they? And calling an evening at Sam's kitchen table a date sounded silly. One thing she had to admit – her time with Craig had given her a taste of what it was like to have someone other than a cat to come home to.

She dug to the bottom of her hamper, pulling out one last blue striped sock. No mate. She tossed it back in. It would just have to wait to get lost in the washer, as nature intended. Her arms over-flowing, she flipped on the basement light with her left elbow and went down the two flights to the basement, stopping occasionally to retrieve items that had escaped her grasp.

She traveled past stacked boxes, some full of her own belongings, others filled with forgotten elements of her parents' lives that she still needed to get to – someday. Maneuvering past the defunct stationary bike, heaps of suitcases, and a 1956 refrigerator, she reached the washing machine, dropping her burden into the big plastic trash can that she used for incoming dirty laundry. Pushing aside the long chestnut curl trying to obscure her vision, she measured out a capful of liquid detergent and turned to the washer. Seconds before she tossed in the soap, she spotted movement at the bottom of the tub.

She gasped. Oh. My. God. There was a small grey-brown mouse doing laps. She slammed down the lid and took a breath. What to do? She reflected with regret that her first impulse, which was to somehow lower Winston into the washer, probably wouldn't work. She lifted the lid again. Two tiny spheres shone up at her. She closed the lid.

Indoor-outdoor vacuum? No.

Maybe a catcher's mitt and a large soup pot? No.

Okay, she thought. There were times when a girl didn't need to be *completely* self-sufficient.

She went back upstairs to the phone. "Hi Sam? I need to ask you a favor."

***

In five minutes Sam had efficiently donned gardening gloves, scooped up the mouse, dropped it into a shoe box, and walked it outside, supervised closely by Winston and distantly by Lila.

"And off he goes," he said, standing on her front walk watching the mouse scuttle under the rhododendrons.

"Probably only to show up in my basement again next week. But thank you, Sam." Her Dad's old army field jacket thrown around her shoulders, she stood next to him in the chilly twilight. She noticed anew how tall he was; at her height it was always refreshing to look up for a conversation. The wish that she had combed her hair before he came over crossed her mind.

"Oh, that's all right. Your suggestions about my diet were such a help that I'm happy to give you a hand for a change."

"Well, you certainly came to my rescue. So how are you feeling lately?"

As they began to walk slowly toward the house, he reached over to straighten the jacket on Lila's shoulder. "Well, I didn't want to acknowledge it, but I'd been having some weakness in my hands this past year, and my memory was beginning to worry me. My health has gotten better now that I've rediscovered the breakfast of champions and started adding more eggs and some dairy to my life. May's death changed my thoughts about my impact on this planet of ours, but I know I have to be realistic, too. I can't do much for anyone else if I don't have my strength. It looks like this man can't live by bread – and vegetables – alone." They both chose a spot on the front steps and sat.

"Glad to hear it, Sam. I don't think the chickens will miss an egg or two, or the cows a little milk." She leaned companionably into his side as punctuation.

He smiled down at her. "Miss Delilah, you've brought some much-needed changes into my life this year. I'm feeling more like my old self and when my time is up at Thomas Paine High School perhaps I'll look for something similar. It's good to feel useful."

"Paine has been lucky to get you. I can't imagine having to deal with Paschetti at the helm, and Mrs. Concepcion looks like she should be on her way to the hospital at any moment."

"It's been good for me to be around other people again. I didn't realize just how isolated I'd become after I lost May. It's been a long climb back and I owe much of my recovery to you." The two friends smiled at each other, amber eyes meeting blue. A moment passed as Lila found herself lifting her face towards his. He took her hand and held it.

"Well."

She glanced away and cleared her throat. "Yes. Well. Thanks again."

He squeezed her hand and gave her a quick kiss on the cheek. "Anytime, Lila." He rose, stood looking down at her briefly, and then walked off to Old County Road with long, quiet strides, his back straight, his hair shining in the dim light.

\*\*\*

She wondered if perhaps she had a serious character flaw. All she had intended to do was to run out for a quick re-stocking of her wine cellar. This was of course a major overstatement. Her wine cellar was actually the rack on top of her fridge, never holding more than three bottles at a time. Regardless. She was out of wine, it was Friday night, and she needed more. Now somehow here she was, against her better judgment, back at Niko's, this time in his entirely too-cozy den. And what an apt name for the lair of a man with such a leonine exterior.

His bulk had filled the aisle of the small local liquor store where she had run into him, bottles of a mid-priced pinot grigio in both her hands. He had smiled and said he had just found a wonderful red wine that was produced at his cousin's winery on the island of Rhodes. He had insisted that this serendipitous combination of meeting her and finding the wine demanded that she join him at his house to share it.

Now Lila looked around at the room, all tans and beige, accented with deep leather couches. She would have preferred an armchair, to create some form of protective barrier, but there was none to be had. Niko sat next to her on the loveseat, the leather cushion making a soft whoosh as it received him.

Unfortunately, she was in one of her after-school ensembles, which were chosen only for comfort, with no consideration to what they actually looked like. She hadn't given her clothes much thought when Sam had come over. She supposed it could be worse - her high-water grey sweatpants with the hole in one knee, or her bleach-stained puce tee shirt came to mind. Still, tonight she hadn't climbed much higher sartorially She cast a quick and surreptitious glance down at her brown jeans and too-tight yellow U Mass sweatshirt, which kept riding up in back. She comforted herself with the fact that at least they were clean.

Meanwhile, he had placed the bottle of wine juuust far enough away that he had to reach across her to refill their glasses, an action that each time seemed to take longer than really necessary. A narrow dish of olives, cheeses, and marinated mushrooms gathered from his spotless kitchen sat conveniently at hand on the gleaming table in front of them. Her glass finally filled, he handed it to her, waiting a beat to take his hand away. She felt a sudden kinship to a gazelle caught on the savannah, mesmerized by its fatal destiny.

"This is really a lovely wine, Niko. And it's from your cousin's winery?" How could she already be on the second glass, thought Lila? Sprightly conversation felt an inadequate protection. "I don't think I've really thought about red wine coming from Greece. Most people seem to first think of Italy or France," Okay, now she was in danger of babbling

"And yet the wineries in those countries are the progeny of Greek colonies established there thousands of years ago. My country grows more than 300 varieties, from Peloponnese to Macedonia. There is much I would like to teach you about Greece, Lila."

The loveseat had somehow become smaller. She could feel the body heat radiating from the solidly athletic form next to her. He was wearing a soft grey pullover with the sleeves pushed up on his muscular forearms. She found herself distracted by the curly blond hair covering them. Trying to find a safer place to focus, she glanced up, only to become locked into the gaze from those hooded silver eyes. Before she realized it, his hand was gently gathering the hair from the side of her head, pushing it gently back as he leaned toward her.

"There must be so much more that I don't know about Greece. I mean, I've never been there, not that I wouldn't like to, I've heard it's so beautiful - and warm – and -"

His lips were warm, too, at first so light, then more insistent, on hers. The couch enveloped her, as did his arms. His body against hers had the heft and brawn of warmed granite. For the first time in a long time Lila felt fragile, desired, and desirous. Maybe it was the wine, or the long months alone, or, whatever. Lila couldn't have cared less. Her yellow sweatshirt was now riding up in places other than her back. His hand moved slowly, but with purpose. Her body responded of its own volition, arching toward him, while her mind was a blissful blank.

She kissed him back, but then, through Herculean will-power, pushed him away slowly. To his credit, he didn't resist, smiling as he moved his arm to the back of the couch.

"I think I may have had a bit too much tonight, Niko."

He continued to smile as he played with a lock of her hair, "Of what, Lila?"

"The wine. It's getting late and I really should head home." She found she was staring at his mouth, remembering its deceptive softness, and how it felt to have powerful arms around her. She straightened in her seat, pulling down the traitorous sweatshirt with a yank. "This was –"

"Too brief. What are your plans for tomorrow? I would like to see you again."

Oh God. Not another evening on this couch. It would be her undoing and she really still didn't know anything about this man. Why had he come to Calvin? What were his plans? Maybe she could take another stab at her detective work if she chose less hazardous surroundings.

"I'm free during the day. Would you like to go for a short hike? We're supposed to have a bit of Indian summer tomorrow."

"Indian summer? What is this?" He tilted his blond head quizzically.

Okay, she thought, this felt like safer ground. A normal conversation. "Oh, it just means that we'll have a break in the cool fall weather. It'll be sunny and a little warmer for the next couple of days. I'm not sure why we call it that."

"Yes, I would like to experience this Indian summer with you. What shall we do?"

"I could take you to Sunset Rock. It's one of the highest points in town and has a good view of the area. Be prepared, though, for some climbing."

Niko looked amused. "I think I will be able to climb to this rock of yours. Perhaps I will even be able to help you."

"Oh, I'll manage just fine. Tomorrow afternoon?" Lila rose from the couch, careful to keep the table between her and Niko, less to keep him at bay than to keep in check any impulses of her own.

She exited the warm golden room, exhaling a breath of relief once she had reached his marbled foyer. Another very up-scale change to the house since the Wetherill days, she thought. Niko opened the heavy paneled front door, pausing and smiling at her before he opened the outer glass door. He stood in such a way that she found it necessary to brush against him on her way out, experiencing a whiff of sandalwood as she passed.

***

In her jammies and knee socks, tucked under an old soft comforter, two bed pillows at her back, Lila felt more like herself. This was what she was comfortable with - her own bed, a mystery by her side, and Winston methodically washing his back leg as he leaned against her. Not very exciting, but who needed excitement all the time?

And yet – there must be some middle ground, some place between a staid life that was comfortable but offering no surprises, and one that produced a sense of standing on a precipice – the way she felt when she was with Niko. Uninvited, the memory of those arms, the sheer bulk of him against her traveled across her mind. Resolutely, she picked up her book and opened it, but did not see the words before her.

# CHAPTER SEVENTEEN

The fact that Lila woke up alone was not exactly a new development that would knock the planets out of alignment, but it was all for the best after the temptations of her evening with Niko. She reached a long arm across the bed to the empty real estate beside her. The white sheet had been laundered so many times she figured she already knew what it was like to sleep on silk. It was just one member of a procession of spotless linens that had been routinely pegged to the backyard line over the years. Her mother may have been an absent-minded artist rather than an immaculate housewife, but she did love sheets that came from the linen closet smelling of sunshine and fresh air.

She heard the tip-tap of Winston's claws on the wooden floor. No wonder he was such a successful hunter; he had the armature of a saber-toothed tiger. He jumped up, settled himself on her stomach and stared at her pointedly. Oh right, she'd shut off the cat door last night. Just as well, or else there'd probably be more than the two of them here in her bed.

"Okay fella. I'm getting up." She grabbed her old plaid robe, technically Craig's old plaid robe, and headed downstairs. She opened the back door for Winston, and returned to the kitchen where she poured herself some orange juice and put on the kettle for tea. She drank her juice and stared out the window, waking up. She suddenly remembered she had that hike today with Niko.

Well, this would be a productive day, she resolved. No more romance, no more staring into those slate eyes, definitely no more kisses, and no more thoughts about running her fingers through those soft golden curls. . . . . The tea kettle's shriek brought her back with a thump. She grabbed a mug, tossed in a tea bag and filled it with water. Yes, today had a definite purpose: to showcase the beauty of Calvin's unspoiled forests and open spaces, changing any thoughts Niko might have had about carving up her town.

***

It seemed to be an ideal day for the hike up Calvin Mountain to Sunset Rock. While not at their peak, the maple leaves mostly still held a generous portion of their banana yellow, several sumacs blazed crimson, and the oaks, now a pedestrian brown, made up for their lack of hue with size. Some of the leaves on the forest floor had the girth of dinner plates.

Niko had picked her up in his huge SUV. She hated to admit that the massive vehicle was growing on her as it climbed the lower stretch of Calvin Mountain effortlessly while cocooning its passengers in leather and heated seats. But everything about this man bordered on the colossal - his house, his cars, his shoulders, his confidence, the very space he occupied.

They had found the trail without difficulty and the day had reached the predicted high of sixty-four, the sun visiting from time to time but absent long enough to keep things pleasantly cool. She could see the wind before she felt it, the breeze first tossing the uppermost tree limbs ahead, traveling hand over hand like an old Tarzan movie until it dropped to sweep over her at ground level. In spite of these idyllic conditions, the going was slow. It occurred to her that rustling through the fall leaves is a charming idea until you realize they are disguising not only the trail, but an endless supply of shifting stones and protruding roots. Add the relentless incline and it was no longer the carefree frolic through the woods she remembered from childhood.

Fresh air! This hike may have begun as just a safer alternative to what might have been his plan for the day, which she guessed could have once again ended in soft lighting, softer music, and seductive wine. Now, though, Calvin Mountain was a refreshing tonic, clearing her mind by challenging her body. Not quite gasping, but with a small stitch forming in her side, Lila mentally reaffirmed her plan to get more exercise, adding the resolution to climb the stairs more often at school. She stepped onto an innocuous-seeming mound of leaves but found her footing give way. She listed suddenly to her left, falling toward a bush with improbably pink leaves. As she fell, one portion of her mind dispassionately wondered what the plant might be while another portion registered the strong hands at her waist, steadying her. She hadn't realized Niko had been walking so closely behind. It seemed this man was forever picking her up. Her mind deliberately ignored the idioms that clamored to be thought, 'being swept off her feet,' or maybe, 'falling for him.' With several pale leaves caught in her dark hair, Lila glanced up to see his head framed by the momentarily azure sky.

Okay. Things were getting way too Technicolor and his hands were still resting on her hips.

"Thanks. I'm fine now. Too many rocks on this trail."

To avoid those hooded grey eyes with the impossibly long lashes, she looked down, shaking out her hair and brushing the leaves from her left side. She tucked a loose lock of hair behind her ear and lifted her head. Before she could think, his lips were on hers while the breeze played around the two of them, their bodies meeting into one. She held him to her as she returned his kiss, then loosened her hold. He smilingly released her but remained enticingly close. "These woods of yours do provide some excitement, do they not?"

"Um. Yes." She took a deep breath, trying to recapture a semblance of normalcy. "All kinds of things can happen here." Damn! What was she saying? "I mean, we have deer and even bobcats in this area." Sure, thought Lila. If she just kept talking, she might forget how it felt to be enfolded in those arms. She was beginning to recognize that at some point she would have to examine her feelings for him more closely.

Her eye caught a blue trail blaze painted on a tree trunk ahead. He continued to smile at her but she stepped forward. "Look – the trail heads this way. I almost took a wrong turn." Oh dear God, she thought, was she going to speak in double entendres all day? Pulling off two burrs from her jacket, she then plunged ahead, happy to put some distance between herself and that last moment.

They traveled on, passing a long-ago farmer's hay thresher, rusting in a tangle of orange-berried bittersweet. The remnants of a stone wall indicated that this area had indeed once been farmed or perhaps used to corral livestock long ago. An all too brief interval of flat land and they were climbing again, and she realized they were at Dragon's Hill. It had been named by the local kids for the shape of a huge fallen tree which had weathered legions of imaginary battles.

The trees thinned as the climb grew steeper, ascending at an almost forty-five degree angle, and Lila was uncomfortably aware of the view she was probably providing him as he climbed behind her. She doggedly scrambled up the last rise and looking up, forgot the stitch in her side, her tired feet, and the temptations of Niko. The entirety of the long valley lay before her, encompassing not only the town of Calvin, but the Connecticut border to her left and the Berkshires to her right. Sunset Rock was untouched by guard rails or warning signs. The granite outcropping simply ended and plunged downward, the next solid land more than a hundred feet below. Lila was visited by the magical idea of being able to simply step out and stroll across the orange and yellow treetops.

"Such beauty. My country has a beauty of its own, but there I have never seen such colors. I have no words for this." Pulling himself up next to her, even Niko was stunned into relative silence. They stood side by side, listening to the wind and the occasional cry of a coasting hawk catching the currents. Suspended there at the edge of her world, Lila considered the concepts of risk and safety. She looked across at the man by her side. What did these moments with Niko mean? Maybe this was what she needed, someone to push her into romance, commitment. She found that she was now holding his hand and it felt warm and strong around her own.

The trip back was anti-climactic, their conversation unremarkable as they descended on the trail. They had discussed how amazing the view had been, and pointed out interesting rock formations to each other. She wondered how Sunset Rock had really affected him. She wasn't sure how she felt about that extraordinary moment on the bluff, and she decided she didn't want to examine it too closely. And she certainly didn't want to provide him with an opportunity to reenact last night's episode.

And yet, this had been a good day, a companionable day. He had clearly enjoyed the simplicity of a walk in the woods, appreciating the simple beauty to be found in nature. Perhaps she was being unfair; maybe he wasn't the shallow opportunist she had painted in her mind. He just had needed to see that the town of Calvin was fine the way it was. And where could this business park Niko was planning go, anyway? The open spaces were becoming more and more precious; without them, Calvin would lose the very thing that drew people to the town in the first place.

At last they reached the field at the beginning of the trail where he had parked. It was still sunny and they were both warm from the hike, loathe to leave the soft breeze for the confines of the car. Lila leaned against the vehicle and pulled her water bottle from the pack she had brought. She took a sip and offered it to Niko.

"Did you enjoy the hike? We certainly couldn't have had a nicer day for it."

"A beautiful day and beautiful company," He tipped his head back and drank deeply from the bottle, returning it to her with a flourish.

"We have other hiking areas in town, not all as spectacular as Sunset Rock, but striking in their own way. That's why we prize our undeveloped land; it's here for everyone to enjoy. And of course, once it's gone, it's gone for good."

"But does the town not need money? All towns must fix their roads, repair their schools. A town needs business. It cannot be all trees and fields."

"I know, Niko. I just worry that I'm going to lose the town I grew up in."

He gazed across the field as the tall weeds dipped in the breeze. "Or it could become even better. Change could also mean improvement if it is done correctly, carefully."

She looked at Niko, his feet planted so firmly in the soil, his broad shoulders squared. He looked capable of taking on the world. "Maybe," she said cautiously.

He turned and smiled quickly at her. "Excellent! We agree! I thought you would see that Calvin could be a fine location for a business park. This would bring money through the taxes. Soon you could have a new library or police station!"

Lila stood up, no longer lulled by the warm sunshine or the gentle wind. "That's not what I meant at all! And this business park that you seem to see as a fait accompli would mean heavy traffic on our roads, wear and tear on our infrastructure! Not to mention the field or forest that would disappear to house it!"

Honestly, she fumed. Here she thought she had gotten through to him, found common ground – no pun intended. All he had been doing was basically casing the joint, looking for likely sites! "I think I'm ready to head back." She tried to open the car door, but it was still locked. So much for the grand gesture, she thought. She was forced to stand there in submission until he clicked the remote and then held the door for her, smiling. She decided his inevitable smile was the most infuriating thing about him.

The ride back would have been silent, effectively demonstrating her disapproval except he had turned on the radio and soft jazz filled the vehicle as it purred down the mountain.

# CHAPTER EIGHTEEN

It was the beginning of first period and Sam was taking a last turn through the school cafeteria to ensure that any late arrivals hadn't decided to hang around after breakfast. With the majority of the student's families living below the poverty line, it was a well-attended meal. Over by the entrance to the school, Anthony Paschetti was overseeing door duty, which had been clogged by a last push of students. He was annoyed this had slowed his morning. The teacher on duty, Mrs. Himmelstein, was dealing with a student needing a special pass, and when he saw she had turned away he quickly disabled the tall metal detector to speed up the process. The crowd was dispersed, and his morning was his own again. He passed by the cafeteria where he saw Sam retrieving a forgotten milk carton and returning two discarded trays to the kitchen. Paschetti sneered at the thought of an administrator who would stoop to doing custodial work.

On the second floor Paschetti interrupted a hair braiding session between two tiny Hispanic girls, sending them on their way, but ignored what looked to be a couple of potential NFL linebackers who were moving at glacier speed down the stairs. He traveled up to the third floor, demanding a pass from a cowering ninth grader, who surrendered it with shaking hand. He returned it, barking, "I doubt if Ms. Ronley would appreciate your dawdling in the hall," and marched off, chest out, master of his world. He passed Maritza Concepcion's office, confirmed that she was indeed there and on the phone, groused under his breath because her space had three windows to his two, and went back down to wait on the second floor.

Meanwhile, on the first floor, the student Leonard Baronoff was pleasantly surprised when he passed easily through the now-disabled metal detector. He handed his school ID to Mrs. Himmelstein, who was manning the desk for tardy passes. After verifying his identity, she stamped his pass with the time clock, and wrote the room number of his destination. He still needed to go to his locker and knew he had to get to class reasonably close to the time on his pass, but still figured he could stall a little by hitting the boy's room for a minute. After all, he'd been suspended for four days, had taken an extra day of his own, and was in no hurry to sit in a chair while some well-meaning adult preached at him for an hour. On the second floor he thought he could see that Paschetti guy near his locker, the one with the beaky nose he was always sticking into people's business. He told himself at least it was someone who wasn't going to give him any real trouble. Nevertheless, Leonard turned around and retraced his steps to avoid passing him.

Having seen Leonard, Paschetti retraced his own path, finishing up in the doorway of Assistant Principal Concepcion. "Um, good morning, Maritza. How are you today?"

Mrs. Concepcion replaced her phone, and turned to her doorway with a smile that dimmed when she saw who her visitor was. "Anthony. What can I do for you?"

"I was, uh, heading to the office for the morning meeting. Would you like to walk down with me?"

"There's a meeting?" Mrs. Concepcion thumbed through her desk calendar. "I don't have it on my schedule."

"Well, you know Sam Fielding. A little slapdash with his communications."

Concepcion stared at Paschetti for a moment. "No, that has not been my impression at all." She pushed against her desk and rose, cupping her pregnant belly briefly. "But if you say there is a meeting, let's go."

\*\*\*

Leonard came out of the bathroom and headed for his locker. It was pretty quiet in the hall that morning; only a few kids were still drifting in. The building would fill up at lunch time, then empty as the less academically oriented decided to dodge their afternoon classes. Concepcion and Paschetti reached the second floor as Leonard opened the door of his locker. "Just a moment, young man," and with that, Paschetti left the staircase to approach the student, Concepcion following curiously behind.

As she reached them, she said, "Hello, Leonard. It's good to see you back," as Leonard turned cautiously toward this adult who was addressing him so politely. In his experience, most of his interactions with adults had been characterized by discord rather than harmony.

"I'm not so sure, Mrs. Concepcion. Come closer and look. I think Leonard needs to explain this." Keeping a safe distance, Paschetti still managed to reach in and pull a large brown envelope from the top shelf of Leonard's locker, opening it to expose packets of cash held together with rubber bands.

"What is that? Nyeht! That is not mine!" Leonard started to reach for the unfamiliar envelope, then shoved both of his fists deep in the pockets of his coat, perhaps to prevent himself from lashing out with them.

"Mrs. Concepcion, would you like to address this issue with this young man?"

"Leonard? What is this, son?"

"I do not know! I do not understand how that got there. It is not mine!"

Realizing that Maritza had not been as aggressive as he had hoped, Paschetti goaded, "Of course it is. It's in your locker." To Concepcion, who was now next to the angry student, "This is the fund raiser money that's been missing."

"Leonard, do you have an explanation for this?" Concepcion reached sympathetically to touch the boy's shoulder. He shook off her hand to reject the kind gesture. For him this was just one more episode in a long line of injustices characterizing his high school career.

"He doesn't have an explanation because there isn't one. First he's out because of fighting; now that he's back he's switched to stealing. His first day back is quite the success," sneered Paschetti. "I think we all need to see Mr. Fielding and perhaps some of our friends in the police force."

Whether it was the mention of the police, or the needling by Paschetti, this was the final straw. Leonard's hand was no longer in his pocket, but had emerged holding a small knife. Paschetti jumped even farther out of reach as Concepcion leaned toward the boy. "Please, Leonard. You are making this so much worse."

Before the besieged student could decide on his next move, Bill Moynihan, who had quietly approached the trio at the locker, came up behind him and embraced him, effectively pinning the boy's arms at his sides. The knife fell to the scarred marble floor with a clatter.

Moynihan picked up the weapon and said calmly, "If that movie in Joyce Ronley's room weren't making so much noise, we'd probably have quite an audience by now."

"Thanks, Bill," breathed Mrs. Concepcion.

Moynihan could have sworn that Paschetti looked more disappointed than disturbed. "Yes, indeed, thank you Mr. Moynihan. It's a sad day when teachers have to know such defensive tactics, but that just shows how unsafe this school has become this year. Not that I didn't have this completely under control," he added quickly.

"Uh huh," Moynihan said flatly. Turning away he asked, "And are you all right, Maritza?"

Realizing he should have said something similar, Paschetti chimed in, "Yes, how are you? Maybe you should go home. In fact, perhaps stay home for a couple of days."

"I'm perfectly fine. Let's just take all of this out of the hall before we do draw a crowd."

With that, the three of them escorted Leonard down to the main office.

Lila stood outside her classroom door as her class rushed out on their way to lunch. Nearby, Bill Moynihan also stood, answering a student's last-minute questions about an assignment. She thought, not for the first time, how lucky she was to have Bill, with his experience and kindly common sense, as her next-door neighbor at school. She looked over to see Warren Brown from her morning class, hovering nearby. Every other teenager in the hall seemed to be on a single-minded trajectory to the cafeteria but he was just standing there, fiddling with his back pack. "Can I help you with anything, Warren?" she called across.

"Uh, no ma'am. Well, I mean, is this your lunch period?" Warren was one of those students raised by a family that believed in manners.

"Yes," answered Lila. "Do you need something?"

At this moment Mary Ann Himmelstein arrived, bearing a steaming container of lasagna she had heated up in the teacher's lounge. Simultaneously, Bill reappeared from his classroom carrying his lunch tote. Seeing the two other teachers entering Lila's room, Warren flushed and said, "No, um, thanks anyway." He gave Lila a weak smile and turned away, walking without hurry down the hall.     Lila watched for a moment, wondering what that was all about, and then turned into her room. She joined the two other teachers in the circle they'd created of student desks.

"So it looks as though today was the end of Leonard Baronoff's career here at Thomas Paine," said Mary Ann, diving into her lunch.

Halfway through yet another salad, Lila watched with a hungry desire she knew was beneath her as Mary Ann took a bite of garlic bread. She refocused. "Yeah, Bill. You were the man of the hour, I hear."

Moynihan unwrapped his ham sandwich and looked up. "Lila, I think it was more a case of the man on site. Maritza is beginning to look as though the big event could be tomorrow – as the father of five, I oughta know – and Paschetti – well, enough said."

"So what actually happened?" asked Mary Ann.

"Well, it was the damndest thing. I was on my way down the hall and I saw them standing at Leonard's locker. It all looked a bit odd."

"Odd? What was odd?" prodded Lila.

"The way they were standing. Or at least the way Paschetti was standing. When I got closer, I could hear him badgering Leonard, like he was looking for a fight. But he was standing a good four feet away. It just looked odd. And then when Leonard pulled out the knife, the only person in range was Maritza. I'm glad I wandered by. I don't like to think what might have happened next."

"How did he get a knife past the metal detector in the first place?" said Lila. "And what's going to happen to Leonard now?"

"Oh, he's out for the year. Fighting in the cafeteria is one thing, but stealing and then pulling a knife on an administrator is another." Lila poked at her salad, hoping to find something more interesting than lettuce and tomatoes.

"Well, the whole event certainly brightened Paschetti's day. He's been strutting around like he'd taken out the entire Gambino family. Not to mention the opportunity to spout off about how dangerous the school has become and the fact that we were missing the money. All since Sam got here, of course," commented Bill.

"Yeah, anything to undermine the competition. As though Central Office would even consider Paschetti for the job," said Mary Ann.

Lila shook her head, "Well, Paschetti seems determined that it's only a matter of time before he gets it. I've wondered what lengths he'd be willing to go to."

Bill looked across at the two women. "I imagine that thought may have also crossed Maritza's mind when she was six inches from Leonard and his knife while Paschetti was standing well out of reach."

Mary Ann zipped her padded lunch bag closed, "At least she'll have something new to think about instead of Ty and Stella."

"Was she asking you, too?" said Lila.

"What do you mean?" asked Bill. "What's going on with Ty and Stella?"

"Oh, nothing, really," said Lila. "At least I don't think so. I think he's just trying to help Stella get through a bad patch."

"Well, he'd better be careful. It can be tricky being a male teacher in a high school. It's too easy for people to read things into the most well-meaning actions," warned Bill.

"I think he's just been a sympathetic ear. Stella's pregnant and trying to figure out how she's going to handle it," said Lila.

"You don't think that Ty –," said Mary Ann incredulously.

"What? No! No, of course not," said Lila emphatically.

"I've gotta say I've seen them together quite a bit," said Bill. "But Ty's a smart guy and I refuse to jump on the bandwagon of conjecture."

"Absolutely," said Lila stoutly.

With that, the bell rang and with it, and their lunch and speculations were over for the moment.

# CHAPTER NINETEEN

It had been a long week in an over-heated classroom. By Friday she was tired of her students and she was pretty sure they were tired of her. She'd dealt with one meltdown (Sasha's boyfriend had dumped her), one near-altercation (Rashawn and Julio in a continuation of ongoing African-American and Puerto-Rican friction in school), and one actual altercation (Stephanie and Bridget – who knew why). She'd exited with the same eagerness as the kids when the last bell had rung.

She had left school so much earlier than usual she avoided the late-afternoon traffic and it was a quick ride home. She could almost sense a decrease in her blood pressure as she approached the center of Calvin. The afternoon sun had drawn the walkers to the sidewalks and the bike riders to the streets. Chatting middle-aged women made way for young mothers with streamlined running strollers. A group of men in colorful form-fitting bike wear whizzed by, enjoying the opportunity to ride three abreast on the quiet main street.

As she drove toward the center she could see Libby coming down the steps of the market; she must have finished her day shift behind the counter. On the right Lila spotted two men in suits leaving Arlene's real estate office. They caught her attention since it wasn't that common to see business attire in the middle of the day in Calvin. It was usually limited to the morning, when the resident lawyers and other professional men were leaving for work. Arlene must have just finished up some high-powered business deal. Lila started to glance away and then her eye caught another person exiting the office. Someone with a powerful build and a head of deep blond hair. Niko. Her car had now passed the office, but by looking in her rear view mirror she could see him stop to shake each man's hand and then slap one on the back in a congratulatory gesture. She remembered her argument with Niko the day of the hike. Had he found a site for the business park? What piece of open space was Calvin going to lose? She shook her head and gave a small pound to her steering wheel as she turned on to Old County Road, literally turning her back on Niko and his land machinations.

She arrived home, and wanting to catch the afternoon sun before it was gone, she quickly changed out of her school clothes into jeans and a soft sweatshirt. She reined her hair into a pony tail and, as a symbolic disconnect from work, left her watch in the jewelry box. Now she needed air – lots of it. Fortunately winter was still holding off and the delay allowed a continuing engagement of autumn. Lila doused the legs of her pants with anti-tick spray to ward off any unwelcome passengers and headed out into the Friday late afternoon sunshine.

The sun was warm, but she still felt the need for her navy and brown plaid wool jacket, and as she left her porch she shoved her hands into the jacket's pockets. She had to step over Winston, who was sunning his ample belly on the sidewalk. Since she'd failed to appreciate his obvious magnificence, he rose and walked ahead, flinging himself down again in her path. This time she relented, leaning over to rub his warm fur. Now that he'd been properly acknowledged he lost interest, and strolled off toward a promising gap in the stone wall at the edge of the yard.

She crossed the road, climbed over Sam's split-rail fence, and cut across the field, which at this time of year was filled with humps of earth and remnants of dried corn stalks. It felt good to empty her mind and just walk, no conversation, no decisions, and especially no people. She was able to momentarily shelve the conundrum of Niko but then thoughts of school filled her head. Every day at Thomas Paine passed at lightning speed as students, each with individual personalities, demands, and problems, departed after fifty-five minutes only to be replaced by another group with more personalities, demands, and problems. This was multiplied six times each day. No wonder the sound of her boot steps over the empty field was so soothing. Enough time out here and she might actually be ready to plunge back into the maelstrom again on Monday.

She thought about how glad she was to have the friendly support of Sam at school. He seemed to be doing well there and she knew she'd miss his presence when Thelma Galaska returned to re-claim the principal's office. Even though she didn't see him every day, it was good just knowing he was there. Their friendship had deepened over the past few weeks, taken on new dimensions. Her mind dodged away from full recognition of what these dimensions were, but she told herself it was simply that they both now had seen each other in a professional role. Yes, that was it. She wondered if, once Sam was no longer part of her working world, he would also fade to the outskirts of her world in Calvin. She realized that the idea bothered her.

She turned at the big oak, a place she remembered from childhood, before Sam and May had moved to town. This tree had kindly grown with its limbs close to the ground, making it easy to scramble up to a cozy sitting spot. She rounded a patch of bushes and red-berried bittersweet and was surprised to see a road that hadn't been there before; it looked newly formed. It wasn't much of a road, dirt with gravel poured over it, but it was obviously being used. This appeared to be right on the border between Sam and Niko's land and led off through the fields toward the railroad line running at the back of both properties. Perplexed and concerned, she stood looking down it until off to her left she spotted a tall figure and headed in that direction.

***

Meanwhile, Sam was contemplating a stretch of his land he hadn't been to for a while. The property line was just . . . here. The scrap of wood pounded into the earth by the surveyor so long ago still wore the pink plastic streamer. It might have once been easy to spot, but the weeds had long ago engulfed it the way they were trying to overtake the old stone wall that separated the two properties. He hadn't been this far back on his acreage for a long time, not since his world had been gathered in like the cord of a bag, tight and small. It had been the constriction of illness, a drawing away from life into May's pain, random sleeplessness, and a regimented schedule of medication. He remembered when he and she had first found this spot so long before. He looked about him, trying to will back that afternoon with May in their fields. The wildflowers had encircled her head as she lay on the picnic blanket, yellow finches in the old peach tree above them. Now the tree was a scarred and ruined stump, almost white from its years in the wind. From it, sharp prongs jutted out, reaching, but connecting to nothing.

He was relieved that the earlier, sweeter memories of their life together had begun to shroud the dark ones of his wife's last year. He also was surprised to realize that when he thought of his future, there was an upbeat curiosity at what it might hold. He knew that much of this was thanks to Lila, and the impact she had recently had on his world.

He turned at the sound of a shout, and saw Lila striding with purpose through the tall grass toward him. She was already talking, even before he could easily make out her words. He caught the finish.

"- and when I looked, I realized I hadn't seen it before." Glossy ringlets of her hair had escaped the pony tail and were being tossed in random directions by the breeze. Pleasantly distracted, he found it was a little difficult to concentrate on what she was saying.

"Slow down, Lila. What are you saying?"

"That road. Surely you noticed it. It's practically on your property."

"Yes. It appears that Niko has created an access to the back of his land. I just saw that myself today. Haven't been back here much, what with one thing and another."

"Well, why do you think it's there? What's he up to?"

"Up to? I'm sure I have no idea – are you suggesting evil and nefarious dealings?" He smiled down at Lila, who was now retying her boot with quick impatient movements.

She looked up at him and decided that he was entirely too good a person. Couldn't he see what was going on? She stood back up to her full, indignant height. "Sam! Honestly! Don't you wonder occasionally what in the world brought Niko here? Does he strike you as a typical Calvinite?"

Sam began to amble back toward his house and said mildly, "I'm not sure there is such a thing. Not everyone here is a farmer. Your father was a college professor, your mother an artist. And not to bring up unhappy memories, but your previous companion, Craig, was a very upscale real-estate agent."

How could Sam be so obtuse? Niko had to be up to something, thought Lila. She followed him, waving her arms.

"Exactly my point! This was too sleepy a town for Craig, and believe me, Niko is even more big-city than Craig ever was. So what's up? Why is he still here? And you know what? This afternoon I saw him at Arlene's office shaking hands with two men in suits!" Lila stamped after him, her long legs enabling her to easily match her strides to his.

Sam paused and looked her, then continued walking. Several minutes went by before he stopped and gazed across to the stand of pines in the distance, "You know, Lila, after the week we've just had at school, I'd much rather spend my weekends reacquainting myself with this world out here in my fields, not looking for problems here in Calvin, too. I've enjoyed working again and feeling useful, but I also need the peace this land of mine brings me."

Chastened, she stopped and took his arm, "Oh, Sam, I'm sorry. I just worry about you."

He drew her hand into the crook of his arm, smiled down into her anxious face, and then turned toward the house, keeping her arm still linked in his. "I'll be just fine, my friend. I might be aware of more than you realize." And with that, they headed off again, the late sun playing across their slim figures as they strolled together in quiet concord through the brown field.

# CHAPTER TWENTY

Friday afternoon hadn't exactly provided the soothing experience she'd been hoping for, what with her discovery of Niko's road and his mysterious meeting at the real estate office. Sam had managed to temporarily talk her off of her high-horse of suspicions, but she still wished she knew what Niko's final agenda might be.

And so far, her Saturday morning didn't look like much of an improvement. Fifty-three essays sat next to her, waiting to be read, commented on, and graded. She poured another cup of tea from the teapot, put her feet up on the coffee table and stared across her socks at the gleaming fall day outside. She promised herself she'd do more than look at it from her couch. Motivated, she took a bite of a muffin, grabbed her red pen and the first twenty-five papers, and forced her brain to focus on the work ahead. With luck and some real power-grading, she'd get half of the pile done and could postpone the rest till later, but a large part of her was still itching to be up and moving.

An hour and a half later Lila was in her kitchen, checking on the split pea soup she'd started. It would provide lunch and maybe a dinner next week and the rest could go in the freezer for future reference. For now, it could simmer on the back of the stove while she took a much-needed break from bad grammar, poor punctuation, and uninspired thinking. Maybe the afternoon grading session would prove to be less depressing since the remaining essays were from a class blessed with several good writers. And she could justify this intermission by getting some photographs of Sam's stone wall and fields. Her classes would be starting Frost soon and many of her students, kids who had never been out of the city, had little concept of the New England his poems described.

She gave the soup one last stir, tossed on her old blue sweatshirt, found her gardening sneakers and tucked her small camera in her pocket. She practically skipped down the steps as the fresh air hit her. A quick walk through Sam's back fields would be perfect. She'd make a point to avoid Niko's new road. Today it would just be her and nature.

Lila began with some wide shots of Sam's biggest field, the one farthest from his house. She wanted her students to experience the sheer size of the space as it sat open to the sky, ringed with yellow and red trees instead of the only view of life many knew, gray stone buildings. The sun was warm on her back and she photographed things that unfailingly struck her as magical: a tiny pink leaf on a moss-covered stone, a patch of scarlet bittersweet, and fluffy-topped grasses that had gone to seed.

Twenty or twenty-five minutes into her task, she was so intent on her work that at first she didn't hear the raised voices at the far end of the field. That sounded like Sam. And someone else. What in the world, she thought? She aimed her camera in that direction and her viewfinder magnified the scene. Yes, it was Sam and he was on one side of the stone wall, Niko on the other. She cut across the wide field and the voices grew more distinct.

". . .historical artifacts. . . original settlers. . .glaciers."

Glaciers, thought Lila? What on earth were they talking about? As she got closer, she could see a conciliatory smile on Niko, and she also recognized the tone she had heard Sam use before with uncooperative students at school when he was driving home a point. They were each on their own side of the old stone wall, over a gap that she didn't remember as having been there before. Frost's "Mending Wall" sprang into her head, and not the part about "good fences make good neighbors", but the description of the narrator's neighbor:

*I see him there*
*Bringing a stone grasped firmly by the top*
*In each hand, like an old-stone savage armed*

Niko certainly looked the part, with his wide stance and powerful shoulders, a rock still in one hand, several others at his feet, and his garden tractor with a trailer in back of him. However, in the poem the man had been re-building the wall, not dismantling it, which looked to be the case here.

Niko's eyes shifted as he saw her approach, but Sam was still unaware of her arrival. ". . And as someone new to this part of the country, you probably didn't know that in the late 1800s, New England had some 240,000 miles of stone walls. Now, of course, we only have a fraction of that number, which is why it's so important to preserve them."

"Indeed," said Niko. "Ah, Lila! Sam was just instructing me on the interesting history of these many rocks I find on my property."

"And why we should all work together to keep them here," said Sam and then as he turned to greet her, "Hello, Lila."

"Ah, yes. We must surely keep them together." Niko's smile was still there, but it looked a bit forced. He had never struck Lila as someone who took direction well. She had always been aware of how different these two men were from one another and now to see them standing there across from each other really brought it home. Niko had on what he must have imagined were work clothes, but they were impeccably clean and obviously expensive. Sam was wearing what she recognized as his favorite field shirt, flannel and frayed at the cuffs, and his faded jeans displayed a big smear of mud across one leg.

"It's good to see you both out working together here. These old walls take a beating, what with frost heaves and burrowing animals." She decided to stay with the fiction that the wall had been going up, not down. "I just came out to take some pictures of it for next week's classes." She pulled her camera from her pocket, hoping to lighten the moment.

"A most excellent idea, Lila, but before you do, I will repair this opening we have before us." Niko began moving the stones back to the wall, and Sam positioned them as they arrived.

Now that a grudging truce had been established, Lila figured she'd better make some use of her camera. She could hear the chunk of one heavy stone against another as she strolled away to another section. She peered into her viewfinder, looking for dramatic angles and making the most of the play of the sun and shadows on the wall. This left her thoughts to wander where they might, thoughts such as how telling it was that Niko hadn't admitted what he was really doing there. And Sam, being Sam, would of course never have pointed it out.

The three of them worked without comment other than occasional clipped suggestions between Niko and Sam on the most effective placement for the rocks. After a few minutes, Lila had more than enough pictures, and realized she was getting hungry. She called out. "I think that's all I need. Thanks for the loan of your wall, gentlemen. My students and I appreciate it." She waved goodbye and began to walk back, this time taking a longer route, following the stone wall's path to where it met the road.

She glanced back once, but the scene of the wall "repair" was now hidden by a clump of wild mountain laurel. Lila walked on and musings about the two men were soon overtaken by thoughts of a big bowl of split pea soup, a toasted bagel, and apple cider.

The roar of a lawn tractor broke into the quiet sounds of her footsteps and it grew louder as Niko pulled up alongside her. She stopped and looked over the wall at him. He looked like some marketer's idealized version of country living, with his shiny new vehicle and his starched work clothes. He just didn't belong here. She still remembered only too clearly how tone-deaf he had been on their hike when she was extolling the virtues of unspoiled spaces.

"Niko."

"I had hoped to catch up with you. I was concerned about our, shall we say, friendship," here he raised his eyebrow suggestively, "when we last parted after our trip to Sunset Rock."

Good grief, thought Lila. All she wanted in life at this moment was a bowl of soup, not a plateful of innuendo. And she certainly didn't want to renew the debate over their differing views on progress. "Nope, we're fine. Have a great afternoon!" She turned and continued walking but was dismayed to see that Niko had now left his tractor and was striding along on his side of the wall.

"Perhaps we could have a further conversation over lunch? I know of a charming place only a few minutes away, with the most wonderful -"

"Thanks, but I just have too much school work to finish and I have some soup at home that I need to check on."

"Perfect! There are few things that I enjoy more than homemade soup!" He swung over a low point in the wall, pulled aside a low branch in her path, and bowed her through.

Try as she might to stay annoyed with him over lunch, Niko had been charming, slicing and toasting bagels as though he belonged in her kitchen. And it was so odd to have him there in the midst of her parents' well-worn furniture and dishes. He opened and shut cupboards, digging out soup bowls and plates, all the while telling her stories of his childhood in Greece. They had sat knee to knee at the small kitchen table and she poured him cider while Winston, the traitor, rubbed up against his leg. As if by agreement, they had skirted around any talk of business or development in Calvin. She also noticed there was no mention of his meeting in the center of town the day before. Instead they compared their travel experiences, although his were more exotic and hers hadn't even taken her to a different continent.

He had praised her soup, and then later sat watching with obvious appreciation as she moved from table to dishwasher, clearing up. When she straightened from putting the last bowl in the rack she found him at her elbow, a half-smile playing across his face. She stepped back, ostensibly to reach the dishtowel looped over the stove handle. She busily dried her hands, and looked over at him with a bright smile. "Well! I'm glad you were able to stop by, but now I must send you on your way. My papers are waiting for me and it will take me the rest of the afternoon to finish them."

He stepped closer to her and took both of her hands in his. It might have been a romantic gesture, had it not been for the red-checked towel between them. "Such a short time together, but such a very delightful one." He drew closer to kiss her, but she managed to slip to the side, freeing her hands and reaching out to open the door.

"Yes, well. I'm glad you enjoyed the soup!" If only he would just leave, she thought. She didn't want to become entangled with someone with such different values, no matter how charming he was. Or handsome. She stood by the door, hoping she was successfully modeling a discouraging friendliness. Niko paused at the door, smiled enigmatically with a "Good afternoon, Lila," and left.

Lila watched through the window to assure herself that he'd actually left and then leaned against the door with a sigh of relief. She was always rattled after an encounter with him. His entirely too tempting physical attributes brought out her baser impulses. That, combined with the fact that they had so little in common made for some pretty conflicted emotions.

Winston bumped against her ankle with a loud "Mmrrow!". She opened the door slightly to let him out and looked down the walk. Niko and Sam were standing there together at the end. Oh God. Why did Sam have to choose this moment to drop by? He probably thinks I've been wining and dining, or at least souping and cidering, Niko for days.

After a moment's conversation, which involved no smiles that she could see, the two men parted like wary cats shelving a fight for some future date. Even from where she stood Lila thought Niko looked smug as he crossed the road back to his place. Sam looked, what? Thoughtful? Sad? He continued toward her house. This day was filling up with too many men and not enough of that serenity she'd been hoping for when it began.

She opened the door further, watching him. He was deep into a traveling contemplation of her flagstones, but then looked up to see her standing in the doorway.

"Hi Sam." She wondered if he would ask why Niko had been there. "What can I do for you? Would you like to come in?" She stepped aside to wave him in, congratulating herself on being a tidy housekeeper and already getting the two incriminating soup bowls and cider glasses into the dishwasher.

"No, I won't disturb you. Just thought I'd bring by this extra loaf of pumpkin bread. Though I imagine you've already had your lunch . .?"

He was digging to find out what Niko had been doing there. Lila stepped out and took the bread from him. "Thanks, Sam. This will be great for dinner later. It'll give me something to look forward to while I'm plowing through my students' writing all afternoon. Are you sure you won't come in?" He did look a bit forlorn standing there on the walk.

"Um, no. Gotta get back and get caught up on all the work around my place that I've been neglecting while I've been at school."

"Is the wall all repaired, then?"

"What? Oh, yes, good as new. Good for another hundred years if no one disturbs it."

That seemed to be the closest reference he was willing to make to Niko's transgression. They wished each other a good afternoon and Lila returned to her house.

Later, on the couch surrounded by essays, she had some difficulty getting her mind focused on the task at hand. It had been an annoyingly pleasant lunch, and even more so since she had been out-maneuvered into sharing it with Niko. She didn't want to enjoy his company, but did, in spite of herself. She also knew she didn't want to be the reason for the look she had seen in Sam's eyes when he had turned to walk away.

# CHAPTER TWENTY-ONE

On Sunday, having raked the entire front yard of leaves for what had to be the thirty-first time that fall, Lila figured she had earned a break. Her day had begun with a virtuous breakfast of oatmeal, not the French toast that was calling to be made from that leftover loaf of crusty bakery bread. Then had come laundry, the dump, and now the leaves. Definitely time to sit on the front steps and just enjoy the air.

She went back inside to pour another cup of tea from the old flowered teapot on the kitchen counter, and on her return found Niko standing in the middle of her walk. He was all countrified up, this time in jeans, work boots, deep purple long sleeved tee, and open dark-blue flannel shirt. His blonde hair was shining in the sun, and the fit of the tee advertised the time he must spend at the gym. Great. She'd been hoping for at least one day this weekend with no complicated conversations. And no temptations.

She noted, in spite of herself, how well those jeans fit his muscular legs. She was beginning to understand the expression of "no rest for the wicked."

"Hello, Niko. How are you today? Could I get you a cup of tea?"

"No, I do not wish to trouble you after your generous hospitality yesterday. But I did want to see more of you. I feel that we enjoy each other's company and, with the right opportunity, could enjoy it so very much more." This was followed with a look that was not exactly a leer, but first cousin to one.

Lila had unfortunately by now taken a seat on her porch step and was forced to look up at Niko, who stood directly in front of her, his knees almost touching hers. She dragged her eyes down to her mug, one that she irrelevantly remembered seeing Sam use the last time he had been over for coffee. The memory crossed her mind of Niko's cavalier attitude toward Calvin's natural beauty the day of the hike, not to mention his disregard for the historical value of his stone wall.

"I'm not sure that could ever happen, Niko. We have such different outlooks and just plain philosophical differences. I look at Calvin and see our woods and fields as irreplaceable green spaces that heal and restore us. You look at Calvin and the only green you see is dollar signs." She took what she hoped would be a calming sip of her tea.

"That is not completely true. I have grown to see the beauty of this town because you have shown it to me. And when I look out of my own windows at my meadows and trees I understand why Sam Fielding and you value them."

"Oh, Sam! That's rich, bringing him into this. You never did explain why you and that man were walking his land. And what about that road you put in that cuts between your properties?"

"I am sure you are able to understand that I need to reach the end of my property easily. It is quite deep, you know."

"Hunh. Do you mean to tell me that you have no interest in Sam's land?"

"Of course I am interested. It is next to mine. And it is desirable since, like mine, it crosses the railroad line that comes through Calvin."

"There! I knew it! You're going to put a business park back there, probably take Sam's land somehow, and next thing we know, we'll have cars and big trucks trundling up and down Old County Road all day long!"

Niko sat next to Lila on the wooden step. He removed the mug from her hand, which fortunately was now empty since she'd been waving it around to punctuate her points. Taking her hand, he said, "Lila. I have no plans to build anything other than perhaps a pool house on my property."

"Then what are you and Arlene Gerrigan up to with your meetings and your maps and listings?"

"Well, if you must know, Arlene has found a new property that has come on the market. It is across town, connects with the railroad tracks, and will not interfere with your delightfully quiet roads."

"And I'll bet it's probably a patch of old trees that we'll never replace or it cuts across our hiking trails." She was damned if he was going to get off this easily.

"No." He smiled at her passion, which she found really infuriating. "It is actually a place where for many years the rail company would dump the ashes from their old coal burning engines. It is wasteland. Good for buildings, but bad for growing anything."

"Oh. Well. So those men I saw you with outside the real estate office Friday afternoon. . ?"

"We were finalizing the purchase. They are representing the owner, an older woman who, as I understand, is happy that someone has found a use for this land." Lila looked down at her lightly freckled hand that was somehow still in his large brown one. She pulled her hand back, trying to regroup now that she'd been proven wrong on all counts. He continued, "And I believe the taxes these businesses provide should help a great deal with the new high school I have heard is needed in Calvin.".

It had been cathartic to work up a good mad. It was more difficult to change gears so quickly into conciliation. Grudgingly she said, "Okay, yes, that would be good." She stood up and looked down into those gray eyes. "I'm sorry I yelled at you. It's just that here you came to town out of nowhere, with your big cars and your money. And you were always meeting with Arlene, and I couldn't get an answer from you that explained anything - "

Niko rose to stand in front of her, his hands on her shoulders. "So we are again friends, Lila Wallace?" The leaves drifting down around them were the same gold as his hair. A more rational corner of her mind pointed out that soon she'd have to rake those leaves all over again.

She glanced down and then across at him.

"Yes, of course, Niko. Of course we're friends," She permitted herself a smile and a small flirtatious toss of her hair.

He kissed her lightly on the lips, and turned her to walk with him toward the road, his arm around her shoulders. "Then we must plan on a proper evening together. An evening with no school the next day or other reasons to rush home." He looked meaningfully at her.

She smiled back at him, enjoying this new idea that she could put her suspicions aside and just enjoy her time with him. No more trying to pry information out of him, no more wondering about hidden agendas. She widened her smile and said, "You know? I think I'd like that, too."

After Niko left Lila settled into the old striped hammock strung up in the side yard. She'd have to take it down soon; summer was long gone – its only purpose this time of year was as a leaf catcher. Winston wandered over and lay in a patch of sun nearby. She swayed gently and stared up into the tree above. Life at home now felt much simpler, or at least it did as long as she didn't think too deeply about how she felt about Niko, romance, or for that matter, Sam.

Later that afternoon she came across Sam in the center of town. He had been dropping off a suit at the dry cleaners next to Arlene's real estate office. Lila had walked to town for no real purpose other than an excuse to enjoy the lovely fall weather. They walked back together, turning as of one accord toward home, the dropping sun at their backs. Lila kicked at a pile of leaves by the road. "So, Sam. It seems I've put two and two together and come up with forty-eight."

He smiled down at her, "What do you mean?"

"All this time I was convinced that Niko was here to swindle you out of your land, or at least to grab some of our remaining open space here in Calvin to build his business park. I've been trying to get him to admit to it ever since he got here."

Sam looked at her with more interest, "So the reason why I've seen

him over at your place - -"

"All part of my detective work, which was pointless, as it turns out. He told me he's purchased that useless tract of land by the railroad tracks out on the edge of town. We might actually have some new revenue around here, and amazingly, all thanks to Niko."

"Really? Well, I suppose that's a good thing." Lila thought Sam seemed somewhat tepid in his approval. "And now you'll be able to stop sleuthing around. No need to spend so much time with him anymore."

She thought that was kind of an odd thing for Sam to say. Unless – he couldn't be jealous, could he? "No, I guess not. I hadn't thought of that."

They walked in silence for a few moments, an occasional car passing them on the quiet road. Lila stopped as a sudden thought occurred to her. "Oh! But I must have some skills as a detective! I've been meaning to tell you. "

"Tell me what?"

"I've figured out that Leonard couldn't have taken that fund raising money!"

"That would be good to know. Somehow in spite of everything, I still feel sorry for that boy. But you do know they did find the money in his locker."

"I know, and I can't tell you how it got there, but he's not the one that stole it. He couldn't have taken it! He'd been suspended; he hadn't been in school for a week. The money didn't go missing until the end of that week, after he was gone. Someone else had to put that money there!"

"Of course! How did I miss that? He's still guilty of assault and I don't understand how he got a knife through the metal detector, but it would be good to at least take the charge of theft off of his record. So, Detective Delilah. Do you have any suspects?"

"Unfortunately, no. Terrence or Roberto have been hassling Leonard since the beginning of the year, but I find it hard to believe they have the organizational skills to break into your office, take the money, plant it in Leonard's locker, and arrange for Paschetti to find it."

They started walking again. "I might have a few ideas of my own there."

"Like what?"

Two cars coming from opposite directions neared them and Sam put his arm across Lila's shoulders to pull her closer to the edge of the road, saying, "I think I'd better keep that to myself for the moment." He gave her shoulders a squeeze before releasing her. Lila wondered if she'd imagined that he'd held her for an extra few seconds.

They continued on until they reached Lila's driveway. She turned to Sam and said, "So I guess it's safe now for me to stop pestering you about your diet and your land."

He took one of her hands in his calloused ones and smiled down at her. "I would never have called your concern pestering. It's nice to know that someone is doing a little worrying on my behalf. It's been quite a while since anyone did. You watched over my fields and even restored my strength. I do believe you've turned that old story of Delilah and Samson upside down."

Flustered for some reason she couldn't explain, Lila could just smile back at him. Then she surprised herself by putting a hand on his shoulder to reach up and leave a quick kiss on his cheek. "All part of the neighborhood watch!"

She turned toward her house, wondering what had just happened. Had she sensed a shift in the dynamics between them? And why had she kissed him? When she looked over her shoulder before shutting her front door, he was still standing there at the end of the walk.

***

That evening she pulled a bucket out from under the kitchen sink, filled it three-quarters full of lukewarm water, and added a healthy dose of fabric softener. She grabbed a big sponge and a wide paint scraper she'd pulled from a box in the basement and marched upstairs. She would wake up to a new view of not only life in Calvin but of her bedroom wall. Beginning with the wall she always saw first in the morning, she sponged it with her tried-and-true solution for removing old wallpaper. She thought about how it was a good thing these walls were plaster, and not some inferior substance that would just disintegrate once she started scraping.

Her thoughts turned to things like this sturdy plaster that might appear to be older and were consigned to the past when newer, jazzier replacements appeared. And yet, like these walls that had held up for decades, they were made of stronger stuff; they would go the distance, they would endure, while the newcomers might crumble like poor-quality sheetrock.

She stood back and admired the empty patch she had created in the sickly green wallpaper. She was now able to imagine a room she might really enjoy waking up to. Truly motivated, she loosened a larger strip of paper, pulling it away in one long piece that reached from head-height to almost her ankles. She looked more closely at the bare plaster. There was something written there in pencil, but still partly obscured. Curious now, she scraped and loosened another strip, pulling this one down as well, revealing a new area almost two feet long.

Still holding the wet length of wallpaper, she stood staring at the wall. There was a large heart drawn on it, embellished with morning-glory vines covered in blossoms. She recognized her mother's artwork. In the center of the heart were the initials K. W. and J. W., for Katherine and James. Her parents must have drawn this on the wall as a young couple, when the family had first moved here.

While being the daughter of such a devoted couple had often been lonely, no one could deny the love the two had shared. It was made of strong stuff and had endured until they were parted by death. Perhaps this was what she wanted, what she'd been waiting for, what she was ready for. Something solid and real, not a hollow substitute, but love as true and enduring as these plaster walls.

# CHAPTER TWENTY-TWO

Lila knew that non-teachers might think having the second hour of a workday free would make for a restful morning. However, in reality it just meant that you wore yourself out running around getting things done and then you had that long stretch of classes still ahead. So far, in the past fifteen minutes she had already schlepped twenty-five *Othellos* to an English teacher who needed them next, and then sat in on a short meeting in the guidance office with a tearful parent and scowling daughter.

Leaving guidance, she saw the figures of Sam and Joyce walking away down the hall. He was leaning down toward her and smiling, and she was looking up at him, her head tilted coquettishly. Lila wondered if Sam had finally succumbed to Joyce's charms. Did either of them realize how unprofessionally they were behaving? Honestly! By now they had turned the corner ahead and thankfully were out of sight. Lila struck the last image from her mind, telling herself that no, of course she couldn't be jealous. What Sam did was his own business.

She continued down the hall, coming upon a couple who must have forgotten they should have been in class. The girl was leaning up against a locker, the boy, who was at least a foot taller, stood over her, one hand on the wall above, the other massaging her shoulder. Just as they were about to kiss, Lila cleared her throat. The girl ducked under her friend's arm and, giggling, disappeared into the neighboring classroom while the boy sauntered off, hitching up his sagging pants as he walked.

What was this, thought Lila? Lover's Lane? She rounded the corner, and still muttering to herself, saw Warren and Stella. They were having a whispered and intense conversation in a dark corner near the auditorium. He was shaking his head and speaking urgently to the girl. She was repeatedly winding her long ponytail around her finger and looked to be on the verge of tears. Lila wished she could stop and explore whatever issue was consuming them, but this wasn't the time or the place. Also, seeing them triggered a thought, so after shooing them back to class, she went in search of Ty Harkasian.

Outside his classroom door, she peered past the reminders to students and motivational stickers that were posted on the heavy glass window. She was in luck; his room was empty of students, and Ty was there at his desk, a pile of papers before him. Taking a deep breath, her resolve firm, she opened the door. She felt a little like the local sheriff, facing off against the bad guy who had ridden into town. Except Ty was no bad guy, or at least she hoped not. She also knew this was a conversation she'd have given anything to avoid.

Ty looked up and then smiled when he saw who his visitor was. "Lila. How ya doing? What can I do for you?"

His desk looked like so many other teachers' desks, piled with books and files in addition to hand sanitizer, tissues, and a jar with loaner pencils and pens. To his left sat his computer, the monitor's edges covered in yellow sticky notes to himself. On the wall next to his desk were pinned school bulletins, calendars, and a faculty phone list. Most of the remaining space held a jumble of signed snapshots students had given him, many of them seniors who had graduated the year before. Her attention was momentarily caught by a particularly beautiful young woman, this photograph larger and more carefully placed than the others.

Lila sat on the edge of a student desk nearest to him. "Ty, I don't know if you were aware, but Maritza Concepcion has been asking some of the faculty about you."

"Maritza? Why? What do you mean? What is she asking?"

"Well, nothing very specific. I think she's curious about your relationship with Stella Slocumb."

Ty's eyebrows were in danger of disappearing into his hairline. "Relationship? I don't have a *relationship* with Stella. She's my student. Would you characterize your interactions with your students as relationships?"

Wishing she were somewhere else, anywhere, she said, "It's just that she's seen you a lot lately with Stella, as I guess a lot of us have. And you know, Stella's pregnant —and - " Scenarios of more preferable locales where she could be traveled through her mind: monster truck rallies, a ten hour rap concert, being trapped in an elevator with Paschetti.

"I KNOW she's pregnant. That's what I've been trying to help her with. . . Wait a minute. They don't think that Stella and I . . . that I'm the father, do they? Lila, I can't believe that you, of all people, are taking the rumor mill seriously."

"Ty, I don't want to listen to the mutterings, but I think some people might be asking why she's chosen to come to you, rather than some other teacher. I mean you might expect her to choose a female teacher instead."

"I told you. She belongs to my church. Last summer on our annual retreat she needed to talk to someone about problems she was having with her family. Her grandmother was sick, her father had left, so her mother had to take a second job. Stella had a lot on her plate. My fiancé and I were acting as counselors for the high school kids."

"Your fiancé?"

His expression softened as he glanced over at the photograph to his left. The beautiful young woman, thought Lila. She hadn't looked much like a graduating high school student, come to think of it.

"Yes. Chloe. We're getting married next summer when school's out."

Imprisonment in that elevator with Paschetti was looking pretty good. "Oh, my gosh, Ty. Congratulations. And I'm so sorry about all this. I'll make it my mission to see if I can stunt the growth of the Thomas Paine grapevine a little."

"You do that. And this is definitely not for publication, but the father is Warren."

Lila came close to falling off of the desk. "*Warren?* Warren Brown? My quiet, polite Warren? I can't believe it."

"Well, believe. He was on the retreat, too, and apparently he and Stella had a 'moment' one evening by the pond when we thought they were tucked away for the night."

"Good grief." She sat staring blankly at Ty for a moment. "Hey, you know what? Warren has been coming by my room, but after hanging around staring at the floor, he leaves a minute later without telling me why he's there. I bet he wanted to talk to me about all this."

"Could be. But I think they're beginning to sort it out. Ramona down in guidance has been working with them. Stella's lucky it's Warren. He's a good kid. I think he really does care for her."

She got up and stood penitently before his desk. "I feel awful, Ty. Can you forgive me for even considering those rumors?"

"Of course. I'm just glad this didn't fester and spread through the whole school. Especially for Stella's sake. So I guess I should thank you."

"Oh please. That's the last thing you should do."

He stacked up his papers and rose from his chair. "I know one thing I'm doing. I'm going to go have a face-to-face with Mrs. Concepcion right now and get this straightened out."

The remainder of her morning had plodded by as she reviewed writing strategies with her classes. The last set of essays had been uninspired or just thrown together, full of what she hoped were careless mistakes. It was too depressing to think that the majority of her students still didn't know the difference between their, there, and they're. She had also returned some authors' papers with zeros. How could the kids plagiarize from on-line sources and then not realize she could find these sites just as easily? She handed back their work and warned them that the next time she would mail the rejected compositions directly to their parents.

Her class after lunch cheered her up a little. More of theses students had actually thought about the assignment. She used the class time to electronically display anonymous samples from the most successful essays.

This was usually fun because while the class expected to see excerpts from Sasha or Gilberto, two of her best students, she also tried to share good work from students who didn't as a rule shine academically. Two of these lit up with recognition when sentences of theirs appeared for analysis, Roberto elbowing the friend next to him while Doreen stopped filing her nails and whispered to the girl at the desk ahead.

Now overseeing the change of classes in the hall, Lila leaned against the old tile wall by her classroom door and zoned out, thinking about Niko, and Sam and Joyce Ronley. She asked herself if she should she be thinking about Joyce and Sam. Was there something to think about? Should she be thinking about Sam at all? And what was the story on Niko? Was this going to be another brief relationship that went nowhere? What about Sam? Was he returning Joyce's interest? Most perplexing, how did she, Lila, feel about any of this?

Kids continued to amble past her, few in any hurry to get to class. Ivelisse, one of her sharpest students this year, came up to her and handed her a stack of books.

"What's up, Ivelisse? We're still working on these."

"I know, Miss, but I'm leaving."

"Leaving? When? Where are you going?" Lila asked herself why it seemed that too often the good ones left and the lemons stayed.

"My family's moving back to Puerto Rico. Can you sign this?" She handed Lila a school discharge form with lines for each teacher to indicate the student's grade and whether books had been turned in. Sadly, Ivelisse's work was so good Lila didn't even need to consult her grade book to look up the girl's average; she wrote A- and signed off on the books.

"I hate to see you go, Ivelisse. It's truly been a pleasure to have you in class. Your next teacher will be lucky to get you."

The girl flushed and said, "Thank you, Miss!"

Holding the books with one arm, Lila used the other to give her a quick hug. "Good luck, sweetie."

Ivelisse took the paper from her and left to say goodbye to the next teacher on her list.

It was now time for Lila to go to her post for hall duty. She went back to her room, putting down the books she'd acquired and picking up something to work on while on duty. The halls were now much quieter as she locked her door. She turned to see Sam, who was a few feet from the third floor railing, overseeing the stragglers on their way to class.

"Hey, Sam. Can't stop to talk. Gotta get to my post."

"Hey Lila."

Lila continued down the stairs to the first floor, passing Maritiza Concepcion, who had been descending more slowly ahead of her, carefully holding on to the railing.

"Hi Maritza. Take it easy on these stairs."

If possible, she looked even more pregnant. Surely she'd be leaving soon. The school would miss her, thought Lila, but they certainly didn't need to make the evening news with a live birth in the hallway.

Below her, she saw Paschetti ascending the staircase from the first to the second, and then he passed her on his way to the third floor. She kept going, telling herself, "Don't engage, don't engage." She was determined not to get trapped by one of his dissertations on how well he would run the school once he took over – that being only a matter of time, of course. Oddly, he didn't even acknowledge her presence. He was a man on a mission. Fine with her.

She heard a scuffle on the stairs behind her and Ty suddenly appeared, running up and then past her, going faster than she had ever seen him move. She turned to see Maritza spinning off-balance and falling forward. Paschetti, almost parallel with Concepcion, was strangely motionless, observing the scene.

She watched in horror as Maritza continued to fall, screaming, reaching for, but failing to grasp the handrail, her free hand clutching her distended belly. Then Ty was there, sweeping Maritza from the air, slamming his back against the wall at the second floor landing. Lila found she was rooted to the stair. All was frozen. Even the generic hallway sounds from below seemed to have stopped.

Then, like a movie taken off pause, movement and sound resumed

Ty continued to support Maritza, who appeared to be on the verge of collapse as he spoke softly to her. Lila ran back up to them as Paschetti slowly descended to the landing. She then saw with relief that Sam was running down from the third floor.

"Sam! Maritza must have stumbled on the stairs. I think we'd better call an ambulance."

"Already on its way." He still had his two-way radio in his hand and clipped it back on his belt. Stepping to Concepcion and in a gentle voice, he said, "Maritza, let's just have you sit right down here until the EMTs get to us." He took off his suit jacket and laid it on the dusty floor.

He and Ty tenderly lowered the shaking woman to the landing. The assistant principal was a bystander, contributing nothing. Sam turned to him and barked, "Get to that hall and make sure it's empty. After Mrs. Concepcion has been sent safely on her way, I'll see you in my office." A menacing looked crossed Paschetti's face, but he turned and went down the remainder of the staircase to the second floor.

"I'll keep the kids on the third floor away from these stairs, Sam," Lila said, returning back to the corridor above. Below her, the two men stood sentinel by the ashen and trembling woman. She reflected that different as Ty and Sam might appear to be, they were really very much alike: compassionate and absolutely trustworthy - men of integrity.

She re-routed anyone wanting to use the occupied staircase, and was glad to see that the ambulance arrived promptly. Mrs. Concepcion had regained a little of her color by the time she was loaded on the gurney, but she was still clutching her belly, a grimace gathering her features. Lila watched as the stretcher was steered into the elevator around the corner from her room. She turned back, not much point in going to hall duty now; the period was almost over. Joyce Ronley was walking up from her science lab on the second floor. She had the gleam in her eye of someone with a good piece of gossip.

"So I hear it was probably Ty who tripped her? No surprise, the way she's been asking around about him and that student."

"What? Where in the world did you get that, Joyce?" Joyce might have her faults — shamelessly throwing herself at Sam came to mind — but Lila thought she was better than this.

"I overheard Paschetti talking to Coach Cleary. He said he saw the whole thing." Joyce sounded less confident of her information and had the grace to look increasingly uncomfortable as she spoke.

Lila looked at Joyce coldly. "He was there but so was I. If it hadn't been for Ty, Maritza could have been badly hurt, and I can't even imagine what would have happened to her baby. He was nowhere near her when she tripped. He ran up the stairs and caught her as she was falling."

Disgusted, Lila went into her room and shut the door.

Her last period class had been a challenge. Normally, she would have been a one-woman-band of activity trying to keep them awake and engaged. Today, she wished they would just simmer down. They had come in eager to tell anyone who missed it about Mrs. Concepcion's fall on the stairs, Mr. Harkasian's flying catch, the ambulance that came, and the police car.

Lila didn't give the cruiser much thought. She figured it was probably normal procedure when an ambulance was dispatched to a school. Anyway, she had her hands full dragging her class's attention back to Walt Whitman. Not for the first time, she toyed with the idea of putting aside the safer poems of the Good Gray Poet for some of his spicier work, but decided irate parents and possible unemployment weren't worth it. At last, the final bell for the day rang and both she and her students were given a reprieve from their efforts. And today was only Monday, thought Lila; it was shaping up to be a long week. She sank into the chair behind her desk and began sorting the day's class work into folders. She heard her door begin to open and was annoyed to see Joyce entering.

"Now before you say anything, I brought you some atonement M&Ms." She placed a large bag on Lila's desk blotter. "You were right; I was being awful. How could have I believed that slander about Ty! We all know what a terrific person he is, and what a waste it would have been to lose him. He's the best looking man in the school!"

Lila smiled in spite of herself. "I'm glad to see you have your priorities straight. And how could you ever have listened to Paschetti? You despise him as much as the rest of us." She poured out a handful of candy. "Good thing these are dark chocolate or I might not have been able to forgive you."

Joyce pulled up a chair and reached for the bag. "Well, if you're still speaking to me, guess what else I brought?"

"What?"

"More news!" Seeing the look on Lila's face, Joyce held up her hand. "Now wait, this is a first-hand account, no hearsay. I was at the main office after they drove Maritza to the hospital. I was picking up more hall passes from Tiana so I saw the whole thing."

"Dear lord, what else happened today?"

"Paschetti! He was arrested!"

"What? You're kidding! I don't believe it!"

"Really! Cops and everything. He was hauled out in cuffs. Probably the first time he's been without his walkie-talkie in two months. I swear, I bet he slept with the thing."

"Joyce! Why was he arrested?"

Joyce pulled her chair closer and put both arms on Lila's desk. "Well! It seems Sam was witness to the whole scenario with Maritza and Ty and Paschetti on the stairs. He saw Paschetti stick out his foot and trip Maritza as she was going down. He called the cops the same time he called the ambulance. They were waiting in Sam's office. Oh, I also learned that Sam figured out how Leonard got a knife into school the other day."

"Sam and I were wondering about that this weekend."

"Mary Ann had door duty that day with Paschetti. She didn't figure it out till later, but she discovered the metal detector had been turned off. It had been working before, and it was only her and Paschetti there, so. . ."

"My God. That's awful. Putting everyone at risk and then later trying to kill Maritza. I can't imagine anyone doing either one. And for a job! At Thomas Paine! That's proof right there that he's unbalanced."

"All I can say is thank you for suggesting Sam to the powers that be. I can't imagine what would have happened around here if he hadn't been the one to fill in for Thelma."

"Boy, you know, you're right. I'm not sure some substitute from Central Office would have caught half the stuff Sam did."

Joyce leaned back, smiling. "You've got yourself a special guy, there, Lila."

Flustered, Lila said, "Me? I don't know what you're suggesting, but –."

"Oh please, I've made no headway at all with that man. And it wasn't for lack of trying. He's all but carved your initials on his desk."

Lila popped a handful of M&Ms in her mouth and was unable to reply.

# CHAPTER TWENTY-THREE

Several days later, life at Thomas Paine High School was finally approaching normal - or as normal as a building filled with hormone-fueled teenagers was likely to get. Students were already wrought up over the upcoming Halloween dance, which meant that harried teachers with over-used patience were eagerly anticipating Friday. As for Lila, it was surprisingly easy to forget sabotage and even attempted murder once she was caught up in the day-to-day routine of teaching. There was nothing like towing a roomful of uninterested sixteen-year-olds through iambic pentameter to compartmentalize her thoughts.

"Okay, so let's see how the accent falls on some names here in class." This brought at least a couple of chins off of the hands they'd been resting on. "Yes, Warren. Let's try you." She wrote his name on the board. "Do we say War-<u>ren,</u> or do we say <u>War</u>-ren? Right. The accent's on the first syllable."

Lila worked her way through several names in class, and the majority was now interested, the students waiting for their own names to be discussed.

"So, Lamar. If iambic is made up of two syllables with the stress on the second, is your name in iambic or not?"

Lamar was pleased to affirm that yes, his name fit the pattern. Lila then paired off the class and put them to the task of placing the accents on four lines of the prologue from *Romeo and Juliet:* 'But, soft! What light through yonder window breaks?'

She was walking through the room, checking each team's work when Stella suddenly grabbed her belly and groaned. Warren, who always seemed to be at her side lately, was her partner and signaled to Lila with alarm. She circled back to their corner of the room and leaned over the girl's desk. "Stella? What's the matter? Are you in pain?" A nod accompanied by a sharp intake of breath was all the girl could manage.

"What's going on, Miss? We've got to do something!" Warren looked up at Lila, his arm across Stella's bowed shoulders.

She crossed the room to her phone and quickly dialed the nurse, "Yes, this is Miss Wallace. I need a wheelchair to room 306. Immediately." She continued with the rest of the information more quietly as she wrote a hall pass.

She hung up the phone and took the pass to Warren, who was now holding Stella's hand. The girl was in obvious discomfort, but the boy, though pale himself, was trying to soothe her. Lila said, "Stella? We're going to get you to the nurse's office right away. It's right down the end of this hall. Warren, here's a pass for you to go with her." The classroom door now opened, and the school nurse entered with a wheelchair. Stella's face was drawn with pain, but she managed to move to the chair. Devontra, who had been sitting nearby, had already gathered up Stella's backpack and purse and now handed them to Warren. The small group left, Warren holding the door and following behind.

"What's the matter with Stella, Miss?"

"Don't you know? She and Warren been gettin' busy," called Maurice from across the room.

She fired her best quelling 'teacher look' across the room at Maurice and said to the class, "That's quite enough, Maurice. And I'm sure Stella will be fine. So how are we doing with those lines? Anyone finished?"

The class ended at last. Any more drama, thought Lila, and we can just skip Shakespeare this year. As she erased the board for the next class, Mr. Dunwoody, the new assistant principal who had replaced Paschetti, went by. He was accompanied by a freshly coifed and lip-sticked Joyce Ronley, who was smiling up at him.

Joyce had wasted no time. The Thomas Paine grapevine had already learned that Dunwoody was divorced, with two boys to whom he was devoted. He was handsome in a pudgy sort of way, and had seemed very pleasant when Lila had met him. Then again, anything would be an improvement after Paschetti, she thought. He had certainly set the bar pretty low for the next person. Any life form short of a reptile would be a welcome change.

Bill Moynihan stuck his head in, "Everything okay? I saw a wheelchair leaving your room last period."

Lila finished writing the homework assignment on the board. "Yeah, I hope so. Stella had a bad turn; I'm afraid that it's the baby. I'll see if I can find out anything after this next class."

Bill nodded and began to leave but then turned back to her. "Oh, and did you hear? M&M says she remembers seeing Paschetti in Sam's office rooting around in the cupboard the day the money went missing. He had told her Sam had sent him to pick something up."

"Yeah, right, after he picked the lock. You know, I saw him at Leonard's locker that day, but didn't realize why he was there. One more attempt to make Sam look bad so he could have the job. I'm just thrilled he's gone. What a slimeball."

"Who's a slimeball, Miss?" Sliding around Moynihan into the classroom, Doreen's dimples were on full display with the idea that she had caught her teachers in a round of gossip.

"You, silly girl, if you don't have last night's assignment." Lila waved at her departing colleague and went to the door to greet the rest of the incoming class.

Lunch had finally arrived. For some reason Lila was absolutely famished today and was more than happy to enjoy the brownies Kashana had brought.

"They're only from a box, but my kids don't seem to know the difference. I figured we all deserved a treat here, too." They were gathered in Joyce's science room and were happily munching away in spite of the specimens in jars looking back at them on the long counter nearby.

"I think they're fabulous, Kashana," said Lila "Way more exciting that my one hundred calorie yogurt and bag of carrot sticks."

"I couldn't agree more, although I really should take another stab at losing at least ten pounds." Chewing her brownie, Joyce shifted in her seat, and adjusted her dark raspberry cardigan, which matched her lipstick. Today she had on a loose twin set that played up her generous frontage while disguising any hint of love handles. Definitely fishing gear, thought

Lila. Poor Mr. Dunwoody won't know what hit him.

"Okay, so let me get this straight, Lila. Paschetti took the money out of Sam's office?" asked Joyce.

"Yeah. I guess it served a double purpose: to sabotage Sam's credibility here and also to goad Leonard into attacking Maritza. To think that I actually saw him setting this up and didn't realize what he was doing."

"Oh please," said Kashana. "How could you know? But talk about Machiavellian."

"Or crazy," added Joyce.

"And when that didn't work, he tried to trip her on the stairs."

"Unbelievable. He's a total wack job," said Kashana.

"I know he's an attempted murderer and all, but on a personal level, I'm just glad he's gone because he was so damned annoying," said Lila.

"Right? Like his morning announcements and the way he thought one afternoon in professional development made him the world's greatest authority on managing a school," contributed Joyce.

Lila searched the plastic container for any stray brownie crumbs. "Well, he's gone now, thank God. Anyone know how Maritza's doing?" She looked up at the other two women, "Good grief, it seems like our faculty keeps ending up in the hospital."

Kashana took the empty container from Lila. "She's doing fine. I spoke with her last night. She's okay and the baby's okay, but she's going to start her maternity leave and won't be back for the rest of the year. They think with all the excitement it could arrive early."

"Good thing we've got Mr. Dunwoody, then."

Joyce fluffed her hair and raised her eyebrows suggestively, "Yes, good thing!"

"Now don't you go scaring that nice man off, Joyce." Kashana laughed and shook her head. "We're still one assistant principal down. We need him."

"Oh, honey. Who says I don't, too?"

Lila smiled and shook her head, "You are incorrigible, Joyce."

"But what I don't get is what drove Paschetti to attack Maritza. She's an assistant principal like him. It's not like she had the head job," said Kashana.

"No, but about a week ago I walked into a conversation with Margaret Daniele and Maritza. Lots of smiling and hints about next year. And I think Paschetti heard it because I saw him on the stairs nearby when I left."

"You know, I've heard from Tiana that Mrs. Galaska may not be back next year. I think she's going to take an early retirement." said Joyce.

"I wonder if she was ever really guilty of changing test scores at her last school," said Lila.

"Oh, that's another thing Tiana told me. It seems that when Paschetti got himself that position there as department chair he fiddled around with the scores to make his department look good. Then Thelma couldn't prove anything and he threatened to put the blame on her. I'm sure after the past couple of years she's happy to retire."

"There you go," said Kashana. "And Maritza will make a fine principal."

"That would work out. Sam could finish the year and Maritza could enjoy her baby for the summer," said Lila.

"You mean you didn't already know? Mmm-mmm. Tight as you two are, girl, I'd have thought he'd told you all his plans," said Kashana. "I've seen the way he's been lookin' at you."

"Not you, too, Kashana. Sam and I are friends. Close friends, but friends."

"Okay, Lila, you just go on looking the other way, but watch it or you might miss out on something good. Meanwhile, any word on Stella Slocumb? Joyce here says she left your room with the nurse."

"Yeah, it's a sad story. I think most of us know by now that she was pregnant. I finally got a chance to call the nurse and it looks like she's lost the baby."

"I'm sorry to hear it. At least one good thing came out of all that. She and Warren look like they've become close. Whether it's his good influence or her thinking about the future, but her work for me has been improving," said Joyce.

"Yeah, me too," said Kashana. "She's a nice girl. I hope she's able to come out of this okay."

"Agreed," said Lila, rising from the lab table. "But for now I'd better get going."

"Good! Not to be inhospitable, but Jonathan said he might stop by after lunch."

"Oh, it's 'Jonathan' already? Well, come on, Kashana. Let's make way for young love." Lila packed up her lunch bag and stood up.

Putting on a fresh coat of lipstick, Joyce looked up from the mirror she'd pulled out of her desk. "You might try a little romance yourself, Lila. I may have had no luck with Sam, but I hate to think about six foot three of good-looking man going to waste!"

On the way back to Lila's classroom Kashana' remarks about Sam kept reappearing in her brain like so much popcorn. It wasn't just the adolescent thrill of knowing someone of the opposite sex was interested in her. Her own feelings for him had been undergoing a shift these past weeks, feelings that she wasn't sure she could identify. Yet, maybe she was done cutting bait and it was time to fish.

# CHAPTER TWENTY-FOUR

By mid-afternoon on Saturday Lila decided Joyce and Kashana were both certifiably nuts. Or, if Sam was really interested in her, as they had kept insisting, he was a world-class master of subtlety. Of course her morning with him hadn't exactly been the best setting for romance. It had started with a joint trip to the dump. Lila had begun to clean out the garage and the oddments left there by her parents. In the process she found that among many other things, she had become the proud owner of a rusted metal bed frame, a broken wooden ladder, and several yards of forgotten fencing. She'd called Sam to see if he and his truck were available.

"Hey, Sam. I have some things for the landfill that won't fit in my car. Would you be able to give me a lift in your truck?"

"Good morning, Lila. Sure, I need to take a few things myself. Let me load up my trash and I'll be over in a few minutes if you're ready to go now."

"That would be great. I'll be ready." She had jumped out of bed early that morning, fired up to get some work done around the house. Since no one but the mice in the garage and Winston on the prowl were likely to see her, she had just tossed on whatever was at hand and charged outside. Now remembering Kashana and Joyce's words from the day before, she thought

213

that it probably wouldn't hurt to put a little effort into her appearance for
Sam. Not enough time for a shower, she thought, but she could at least
comb her hair and change into something other than the ripped sweatshirt
she had been working in. What the heck, maybe she'd even put on a little
make-up.

She had just tossed on a soft gold fleece that brought out the amber in
her eyes when she heard Sam's horn in the driveway. She brushed her hair,
put it up with a tortoiseshell clip, and ran downstairs. Together they loaded
the truck and she climbed up into the cab next to him. Lila decided this was
kind of nice on a cool autumn morning, bouncing along in the old truck,
Sam by her side. The radio was playing a song by Lyle Lovett and the sun
shone in warming the cab, a good thing since the truck's heater had seen
better days. They arrived at the dump and unloaded everything – relegating
the fencing and bed frame to the metal heap and the ladder to the
recyclable wood pile, then dropping Sam's trash into the compacter.

"How about I treat you to a late breakfast in payment, Sam?"

"I'd like that a lot. I already ate earlier, but I wouldn't turn down a cup
of coffee."

"Let's go over to that coffee shop down the road. I still haven't eaten
anything and I'm famished."

They pulled into the small parking lot, luckily grabbing the last spot.
Sam opened the gingham-curtained door and they entered a crowded room
abuzz with conversation and fragrant with the aromas of fresh cinnamon
rolls, bacon, and coffee. Lila waved to Toby Giavanelli, sitting with three
small versions of himself in descending order of ages. He must be giving his
wife Toni the gift of a quiet morning by taking their boys out for breakfast.

They were all sticky and smiling, happily working their way through stacks of pancakes. She and Sam found a table for two wedged under a window, and there was just barely enough room for them to slide into their chairs. The one waitress, middle-aged and generously proportioned, was maneuvering gracefully through the packed room. She turned toward them, automatically filling Sam's coffee cup with one hand as she placed menus on their table with the other.

"I don't even have to look at a menu. I know exactly what I want. How about you, Sam?"

"Those cinnamon rolls had me as soon as I stepped in the door."

Lila turned to the waitress, who was still holding the coffee pot. "I'll take a stack of pancakes with two eggs, sunny-side up."

Sam said, "I guess you did work up an appetite." To the waitress he said, "Just one of your cinnamon rolls for me."

She smiled and said, "You got it, honey," and bustled off to put in the order, pouring out coffee refills on her way.

It seemed odd to be in a restaurant with Sam, even if it was just a local joint with neighbors calling across the room to each other. She shifted position and her knee touched his. With their long legs and the limited room it was difficult to avoid. She said, "This is nice. It's been a crazy week at school. I think we both needed this weekend. And word has it that you'll be staying on at Paine until the end of the year?"

"That's right. I'll see what I can do to hold things together until Ms. Concepcion takes over in the fall. We got off to a pretty rough start, but I think it'll settle down now."

"And I think it will be good for the school if you stay. We can't keep changing leadership in the middle of a school year. The students – and the staff – need some kind of consistency." She smiled across at him, "Plus, I like having you there." There, she thought, she'd handed him an opening. Let's see if Joyce was right about his feelings.

He nodded in agreement. "And I like being there. I'd forgotten how much I missed the world of education. There's all the bureaucratic nonsense, and troubled students, and worried parents, but there's more to it than that. Some people may see it as a cliché, but we really do make a difference in someone's life every day. Not many jobs where you can say that."

Well, that fell flat, she thought. She was as dedicated as the next teacher, but she had hoped to have this develop into more than a conversation about the wonders of teaching. Thankfully, their food had arrived and Lila concentrated on her breakfast while Sam talked about the characteristics of the perfect sticky bun.

Back at her house, Lila turned in the truck to Sam. "Thanks. I'm glad to get some of that old stuff cleared out. It's good to get a fresh start on things and it's easier when you can put away the past."

He looked back at her, a half-smile playing at his mouth. He paused and then became his hearty self again. "Indeed. Let's hear it for fresh starts. Nothing like an empty garage to give you a new lease on life."

"Yeah, maybe I'll celebrate with some spackling or get really festive and clean out the gutters." This was hopeless, she thought. The man was completely tone-deaf to romantic suggestion. She'd give it one more try.

"So, what about you? Any plans for today – or tonight?"

"Nope, nothing much. I brought home some paperwork, but after that I think I'll spend some time out in my fields, make sure they're ready for winter."

"Okay then. Well. See you at school." Lila slid from the truck, shut the door and went to her house without a backward look.

She spent the afternoon in a cathartic flurry of activity, vacuuming, straightening, dusting. Winston repeatedly tried to settle into a location and then found that he was in the epicenter of commotion, so he finally slipped out of the cat door for the quiet of the outdoors. Lila muttered and dusted, and muttered and polished. "Honestly! It's hopeless. And what was I thinking? Why did I even listen to Joyce? To Kashana? He doesn't give two hoots, all he wants is a buddy, someone to keep him company!" She punched a pillow. Okay, fine! Time to get on with life! She reached over to where she'd left her phone and found the new number in her contact list.

\*\*\*

At seven p.m. Lila stepped into her black heels – the low ones, it wouldn't do to be taller than Niko. She turned to look at herself in the tall oak mirror. Not bad for a school marm. She had gone for broke and decided to wear her never-fail, knock 'em dead, red sheath. If Niko had been surprised when she called him, he had hidden it well. How fortunate that she had called, he had said. There was a new restaurant he had been

wanting to try, very elegant, very romantic. She'd almost been able to see
his raised eyebrow, his seductive smile. Fine with her. A dimly lit restaurant
with murmured conversation and a companion with a not-so-hidden
agenda would be a refreshing change from the wholesome life she'd been
leading.

She opened her door to Niko's knock; the sleek sports car waited
behind him in the drive like a partially tamed animal.

"Hello, Niko. I'm so glad you were free this evening. It'll be nice to
have an evening to talk and get to know each other a bit more."

After looking appreciatively at her dress, rather than answering, he
pulled her to him and kissed her. All thoughts of going anywhere were
momentarily swept from her mind as waves of desire cascaded through her.
Her knees gave way slightly but his arms were firm around her. She took a
deep, cleansing breath and stepped back, reaching blindly for her coat
where she had left it on the stairs' newel post.

He took her coat, gently draping it about her shoulders as he breathed
into her ear, "As soon as I saw you I knew that was the only possible way
for us to begin this evening. You are lovely, Lila." She didn't usually see him
in a suit and tie; he really was a magnificent specimen. The well-cut jacket
still showed indications of the powerful body beneath it. She regretfully
wrenched her over-active imagination away from the steamy direction it had
been headed. She'd at least try to control herself long enough to make it
through dinner. Then, who knew?

"Thank you, Niko. But we should probably be leaving – didn't you say
we have a reservation for eight?"

"Yes, I am sad to say. But this is a restaurant that I think you will enjoy and I know that I will enjoy watching heads turn when you enter."

Lila was thankful that Niko had chosen the sports car for the evening, instead of his SUV since shifting gears kept his right hand occupied. As it was, his hand still had a tendency to stray in her direction. They traveled into the evening, soft jazz on the radio and the low roar of the engine filling the interior of the car. Down quiet country roads, through a neighboring town's center, and then they came up to a restaurant on the outskirts. A hand-carved sign with grape leaves proclaimed in gold lettering, *Yia-Yia's Kitchen*. It was obviously popular; the parking lot was almost filled to capacity and many of the cars looked to be luxury vehicles. This must be a very upscale place indeed, thought Lila.

"I didn't even know this was here, Niko. How ever did you discover it?"

"A gentleman I met while looking for a suitable site for my business park told me of it. When he realized that I am Greek he insisted I must try it."

He opened the restaurant door and they entered into an interior filled with the soft clink of silverware, snowy tablecloths, muted conversation and subdued lighting. An unseen piano played in the background. The hostess walked them to a table that looked out over a courtyard that even this late in the season still held some plants, strategically lit by dim lights hidden here and there.

Glancing out, Niko said, "I understand that they grow many of the herbs and greens for their menu here at the restaurant. I hope you will enjoy it."

It certainly felt very luxurious. It would be easy to grow accustomed to dining this way all the time. Lila wondered for a brief moment what a life with Niko would be like. Would it be all four-star restaurants and exotic locales? She picked up the heavy menu adorned with gold braid. A silent waiter materialized by her side and filled their water glasses. She smiled across at Niko. "It all looks wonderful. Now you must help me to order."

It had been a long time since Lila had enjoyed an evening like this. They had begun with mezes of saganaki, thyme-crusted Greek cheese with Metaxa and they also shared an order of kefte mentite, chopped meat and yogurt patties. Lila feared she may have overdone it with the appetizers, and was thankful she had ordered a simple dish of grilled fish, flavored with olive oil, lemon and oregano. Niko chose arni youvetsi, a braised lamb shank served with feta cheese and tomatoes, and seemed none the worse for wear. The was a man with big appetites, she told herself. Her thoughts tended to stray to those other appetites as they worked their way through a very good, and probably very expensive bottle of wine.

She found she was spending more time watching Niko's mouth as he told her of his youth in Greece than she did actually listening. Lila smiled at him as he poured her another glass of wine. He really was a very attractive man, very attractive.

# CHAPTER TWENTY-FIVE

A beam of sun had found its way around the deep green roman shade and it felt to Lila as though its next goal was to pierce a hole in her left eyelid. What time was it? She turned her head – whoa! The stabbing pain above her left eyebrow told her that moving to search for a clock in this unfamiliar room may not have been a good idea. A heavy brass clock on the highly polished tiger maple bedside chest showed nine a.m.

She closed her eyes, thinking that perhaps if she just went back to sleep, the next room she'd see would be her own. However, unfortunately all that happened was that she was now more aware of the unfamiliar feel of the sheets – Egyptian cotton? About two thousand thread count? And more aware of the unfamiliar smells – clean, woodsy, but definitely masculine. And more aware of sounds.

She heard a footstep and then the door, which had been slightly ajar, creaked slightly as a wooden tray entered, followed by Niko, who was in pajama bottoms and nothing else. Looking across the antique Turkish carpet at the man before her – the golden chest hair, the flex of his arms, the width of his shoulders – she could understand, with an inward shudder of pleasure, how she had ended up in his bed. And especially what had happened once she got there.

Niko placed the tray next to the bed and sat down on the duvet. She found she was mesmerized by his mouth as he unleashed his smile, one hand solidly placed on either side of her. She quickly rubbed under each eye, hoping to erase any semblance of raccoon from the previous night's mascara, and then pushed her hair back from her face. How was it, she thought, that everyone in movies wakes up dewy-eyed, make-up intact, with breath that would make a hygienist proud?

"And how are you, this lovely morning?" Niko gently pushed aside a strand of her hair that had fallen across her forehead.

"Um fine." She licked her lips, wondering how it was he was unable to hear the warring voices bellowing to her in her head, one shouting: 'Look at this guy! And here's the bed, all warmed up!' and the other screaming: 'WHAT are you doing? Go home, where life is simpler, understandable!'

"I am so very, very pleased that you are here." His voice had taken on a deeper tone and he began to lean toward her.

She pushed herself up and back onto the pillows. Whoops! Not a good idea. She was suddenly very aware that yes, she was covered, but just barely, by the black camisole she had worn the night before. She didn't feel particularly alluring, but his gaze proved he had a different interpretation. She turned instead to the tray he had brought, "So what do we have here? Fresh strawberries? And coffee. Thank God. Coffee." Tea was her usual morning kick-starter, but today her system definitely needed something stronger. She reached for the mug in front of her.

Smiling again, he sat back and said, "Yes, you did seem to enjoy the wine we had last night. And I enjoyed the rest of the evening, as I hope you did."

Oh, lord, she thought. She certainly had. It had been astounding, incredible. *He* had been astounding, incredible. Looking across her mug at the tousled hair that had been so soft in her fingers, she took a soul-restoring sip and put it back on the tray. "It was wonderful, Niko. The restaurant, the wine, the music – and after."

Now he was leaning toward her, cupping her shoulder in his hand as he kissed her. Unable to resist, remembering the night before, she returned his kiss but then regretfully pushed him back. She took a deep breath. "Niko."

The corners of his mouth twitched up. "Lila."

She sat looking at him. Their physical connection was compelling, but emotionally it felt hollow. She thought she had had both with Craig, and yet she had been unwilling to consider their life beyond the day to day. Niko was a man of the moment, ephemeral. Given her history, he should have fit comfortably into her pattern for short-term liaisons. He placed the tray on her lap and popped a strawberry into his mouth. God, she thought, he was even sexy chewing fruit. "I think. . . I think I should be getting home."

He paused, his head tilted slightly. "Why don't you drink your coffee, and I shall take a shower." He rose from the bed. "Unless perhaps you would care to join me?" He smiled at her from the doorway.

"No, thanks. I know where that would lead. I think I'll finish my coffee and wake up a bit."

"Very well. Disappointing, but I do have a meeting in the city for which I should prepare. It would be my pleasure, though, to drive you to your house on my way."

He certainly seemed to have bounced back from her rejection. She sat back against the pillows, berating her own stupidity and congratulating her resolve.

***

She was finally at home. The parting with Niko had been, if not terribly romantic, good-natured, and he had signaled an offer for a repeat of their evening whenever she might wish. At this point, she couldn't say whether that would happen. Niko didn't appear to be burdened with romantic longings. It had been an enjoyable evening, nothing more. For now, she was thrilled to just soak alone in her tub while Winston, after forgiving her for abandoning him all night, washed himself on the bathmat. She scrunched down in the warm water to cover her shoulders and stared at her knees.

The past few weeks had given her a lot to digest and her world seemed to be filled with paradox. Anything but a confused retiree, Sam had exhibited the strength to lead a school and bring Paschetti to justice. Also, how could she have misread the signs about Ty and Stella? Maybe Paschetti was an infection that had somehow tainted the whole atmosphere at school, her deductive powers included.

No, things had not been as they had appeared. Look at Niko. She had convinced herself that he was plotting to acquire Sam's land, when in reality he had only been trying to improve his own. The office park that she had thought was such a threat was actually going to benefit the town, and would provide jobs and capital while using fallow land, not Calvin's fields and forests. Add to that, she had believed that Sam had gone all starry-eyed about her!

She had misread everything – Sam, Niko, Ty. Frustrated and disgusted, she submerged and the water lapped at the edge of the tub. Winston rose in protest at the unexpected spray and stalked from the room.

Cleansed both bodily and mentally, all thoughts of the night with Niko firmly banished from her mind, she decided that what she needed was wholesome physical labor. She jammed an old Red Sox baseball cap on her head and zipped up the fleece jacket she used for yard work. No one she needed to impress. Outside, she stood on her porch and surveyed the yard. The final leaves were down, not really enough for a serious raking session, but enough to make things look messy. Instead, maybe she could grind them up with the riding mower. It had been her father's and was moody at times, but she was pretty sure she could conquer its headstrong ways.

She was backing it out of the garage when she saw Sam on his way down her drive. His stride was long, like his legs, and he smiled broadly when he saw her. For a ridiculous moment, Kashana's words from the other day darted across her mind: "the way he's been lookin' at you." She felt her chest constrict a little. Sam had always been an element of her world, a neighbor, a friend, and to think of him romantically was foreign, but somehow warming. She realized that she always felt better when she saw him. She was suddenly aware of her haphazard wardrobe choices for that day.

The mowing plate on the machine was still raised, so it wasn't quite as noisy as it could have been, but they still had to talk loudly to hear each

225

other.

"Hey Lila. Did you think the grass has had an autumn growth spurt and needs cutting again?"

"No, just getting rid of the last of these leaves."

"Stopped by earlier, but you must have been sleeping in."

Yeah, thought Lila, but not here. "Uh, yeah. Must have missed you. Anything up?"

"Like to come over for dinner later?"

Should she? Were she and Sam just going to have endless dinners, alternating between the houses until they were too old to hobble back and forth? It occurred to her that she wanted something more with Sam, but wondered if he'd ever be able to move beyond the death of his wife May. She realized at that moment that she wanted more than friendly dinners with Sam but the chances of their moving forward looked bleak. She decided she may as well just stop all this once and for all. She shook her head. "I don't think so. I'm going to get this mowing done and have a quiet evening."

His shoulders sank a little, but, always polite, he nodded and smiled. "Sure. That's fine. . . Guess I'll get back, then." He turned and walked slowly away down the drive.

Lila turned the mower to start on the back yard. The path around the garage to the back was narrow, with a drop-off into the woods on the side. Unconcerned, she continued on her way. She had mowed this yard more times than she could remember and she was well familiar with its idiosyncrasies. It was damp on this side of the garage, and soft moss, rather than grass, grew in abundance. Good thing, too, that she never had to cut here, thought Lila, since without much sun it was also damp and therefore slippery.

Her mind was still turning over her relationship with Sam, forbidding her to look the other way, as she had for so long. Was the disappointment she saw in his eyes simply due to the loss of an evening's companionship, or something more? She would have liked another evening with him to explore this idea and she regretted the answer she had given him. Was she ever going to be able to get things right?

She gave the steering wheel a yank of annoyance at her own bungling. The mower responded eagerly, veering to the right, and therefore, toward the tangle of brush, vines, and trees below. Disbelieving that this was happening, she gripped the wheel with both hands as she and the mower slid sideways over the edge. An outreaching branch pulled her cap from her head while another scraped her cheek. It was only about a three-foot drop but wedded as she was to this roaring machine, it seemed like a trip down a bottomless chasm.

The motion stopped, but not the noise. The mower was roaring now. It had wedged against a tree, which took most of the weight, but her right leg was trapped by this same tree and she had no idea how to extricate herself. Well! she thought. This was just perfect. She had turned away Niko, then Sam, and now she would die here alone, within sight of her own house. Her lifeless body would be visited only by deer, woodchucks and Winston. The toll of minimal sleep and a good dose of self-pity overtook her and she felt a tear roll down her cheek, stinging her where the branch had scraped it. Correction, she thought: her lifeless, disfigured body.

"Lila? Lila!" She looked up to see Sam skidding down the

embankment to her.

"Oh Sam!" she yelled over the machine. "It slid down and my leg's caught and I can't get it out."

"Can you lean on it?" he yelled back.

"Huh?"

"Your leg. Can you lean on your right leg?"

"I guess," Lila shifted her weight, lifting her slightly from the seat of the mower. It was suddenly blissfully silent.

"Most mowers will shut off automatically when there's no weight on the seat." Sam circled around to stand next to her. "Okay, now I'm going to push it up on this side – enough, I hope, for you to pull your other leg out. Ready?"

"Yes."

Sam braced himself and pushed the mower away from the tree until Lila, hopping on her right leg, was able to extricate the other. As he released the mower, it fell back with a thump and he pulled her clear.

His arms still around her, he looked down. She was uncomfortably aware of her snarled hair and bleeding cheek.

She found to her annoyance that she was crying again. "Oh, Sam. That was awful." She wiped her running nose with her hand. "What would I have done if you hadn't been here?"

"Well, I was here, wasn't I?" His blue eyes had a different light in them, she thought. One she didn't remember seeing before. He removed a twig from her hair.

She looked down, finding it was easier to talk into his soft blue flannel shirt. "Sam, I'm sorry. I'd like to have dinner with you if you still want to. It's just that I didn't know how you really felt, and I wasn't sure how I felt, and Joyce Ronley said –"

He put a finger under her chin, lifting her face toward his.

"To hell with Joyce Ronley and to hell with dinner." And with this, standing in a pile of brush, the mower giving off the occasional shuddering clank, he pulled her to him and kissed her.